SHAWNEE

THE ADVENTURE BEGINS

SHAWNEE

THE ADVENTURE BEGINS

BOB GIEL

HAT CREEK

HAT CREEK

an imprint of
Roan & Weatherford Publishing Associates, LLC
Bentonville, Arkansas
www.roanweatherford.com

Library of Congress Cataloging-in-Publication Data
Names: Giel, Bob, author
Title: Shawnee/Bob Giel | Shawnee #1
Description: First Edition. | Bentonville: Hat Creek, 2021.
Identifiers: LCCN: LCCN: 2022934303 | 978-1-63373-758-7 (trade paperback) | ISBN: 978-1-63373-760-0 (eBook)
Subjects: FICTION/Westerns | FICTION/Action & Adventure | FICTION/Thrillers/Historical
LC record available at: https://lccn.loc.gov. LCCN: 2022934303

Hat Creek trade paperback edition June, 2022

Cover and Interior Design by Casey W. Cowan
Cover art by Charles M. Russell (1864-1926)
Drifters, 1892, Watercolor on paper
Editing by George "Clay" Mitchell & Amy Cowan

Some ten years before he created characters like Spiderman, the legendary Stan Lee produced a western comic called Kid Colt, Outlaw. It was 1949. I was nine-years-old and already caught up in the Western genre. Extensions of the B-Western movies I frequented could be found in their comic book versions at the local newsstand. Each month, a new edition. I couldn't wait.

Then Kid Colt showed up. This one was different. It had a back story that put the wronged Kid on the outlaw trail, hunted, constantly running. But along the way, he'd stop to help folks in need, putting himself in danger of capture or death. The books had meat to their stories, tension, suspense.

Now, I'm fortunate in the fact that I look a bit like Stan Lee. By growing a mustache, combing my hair straight back and dressing in similar outfits, I've been able to pull off credible, but respectful, impersonations of Stan at comic conventions. It's become my personal connection with a man I've come to admire deeply.

Fast forward to 2017 and the search for the main character of my next novel. Random visits to comic book stores, (yes, I still read them), unearthed a couple of old Kid Colt comics. I bought them and everything clicked. I had the character. Shawnee was born. Thank you, Stan, for that inspiration.

I humbly dedicate this book and its sequels to the man whose contributions, not only to the comic book world, but to the world in general, have been monumental, the late Stan Lee.

Excelsior!

Acknowledgements

WHILE THIS BOOK WAS A labor of love for me, other minds contributed to its completion. The contributions of developmental editor, George "Clay" Mitchell has been invaluable in making this more a more cohesive and more reader-attractive volume. Amy Cowan's insightful line edits got much more right than just the language. Both must be commended for work above and beyond the call, and they have my undying gratitude for their efforts.

The entire Oghma Creative Media family, led by Casey Cowan, have been essential to my development as a writer as well as the light at the end of my tunnel.

As always, my own family's help and support are vital to my success, and are herewith acknowledged. I am truly blessed.

1

I N THE MIDDLE OF THE central Kansas plains, a rider moved southwest, alone on a relentless journey. There were things behind him that needed to stay behind him. To ensure that, he needed to keep moving, keep running. The recent past hung heavily on his mind. It had all happened so fast his head still swam from it, but he had to keep his wits about him. This was a life or death matter of survival. If he stopped or even slowed, he could face the wrath of Carl Teverence and the Jayhawkers before he was ready. He'd allow the encounter sometime, when he was better prepared to prevail, under circumstances he controlled.

Until that time came, he kept moving. Uncertain of whether Teverence was trailing him, he felt it prudent to put as much distance between himself and the Shawneetown vicinity as possible while he was still fresh. His days were filled with steady riding, stopping only for food and water and to care for the horse. Nights were spent in whatever secluded campsite he gauged would afford him protection from the elements and offer cover from attackers, two or four-legged variety. He slept with his new constant companion, the Navy Colt, always within easy reach.

After a week on the trail, he found Toby Joe Hawks's estimate of the length of time the food would last to be accurate. Lon now guessed he had enough to get him through two more days before he would need to replenish. His water supply was waning as well. With no streams in sight, he began to keep an eye peeled for the nearest settlement.

Cresting a slight rise during mid-morning, he came upon what appeared to be a farm in the distance. He saw a house and a barn, and, without hesitation, he set out for the place. As he approached, he noticed the buildings were in need of maintenance. There appeared to be no activity at all. Had the place been abandoned? He slowed his horse and entered the area carefully, moving to the house and drawing rein. "Hey, anybody in there?"

No answer came. There was only stillness and the sound of the wind off the plains. He glanced around. The barn door was closed. Maybe they were in the barn and unable to hear him. Pulling his mount around, he directed the animal to the barn door and called out again. Only silence answered him. He dismounted and went to the door. From the hayloft above him, a brushing sound reached his ears, loud enough to be heard over the wind. By the time he looked up, the origin of the sound, a two string bale of hay, had fallen halfway down. Frantically, he tried to move the horse to get out of the way and, at the same time, deflect the object, but he was not fast enough and was dealt a glancing blow as the bale crashed to the ground. He was thrown from the saddle to the ground and stunned. It was enough to knock the wind out of him. Disoriented, he blacked out.

———————

"HEY, MISTER, ARE YOU EVER going to wake up?"

The voice seemed distant as Lon slowly regained consciousness. He opened his eyes to see the blurry image of a child, a girl maybe.

The pitch of the voice gave him the clue, but the figure was not clear enough yet to tell for sure. Blinking his eyes helped, and, within seconds, he made out a girl in a rumpled gingham dress. He estimated her age at about eleven or twelve. She had a round, cute face and stringy brown hair reaching below her shoulders. Hunkered over him, the child studied him intently.

He tried to move, learning only then he was on the ground with his hands tied behind his back. "What the—" An attempt to pull free failed. Puzzled, he stared at his apparent captor.

She stared back. "Are you hurt?"

"What's going on?" Lon growled. "What'd you do here?"

"I'm sorry. I didn't mean to hurt you. I just wanted to stop you."

Still perplexed, Lon studied the child. "Stop me? From what?"

"From leaving."

Lon shook the cobwebs from his brain and tried to grasp what was happening. He glanced around to see the hay bale which he now remembered falling from above him and hitting him. "Did you push that there bale on me?"

"Yes. I couldn't think of anything else to do to stop you."

"You ever think to maybe ask me not to leave?"

"Yes, but how could I stop you if you said no?"

"So, you knocked me down with a forty-pound bale I still ain't sure how you moved, and you trussed me up like a lamb for the slaughter?"

The girl made a face indicating embarrassment. "I couldn't think of anything else to do. You're not hurt, are you?"

Lon made a quick assessment. "I reckon not."

"Good. I didn't want to hurt you."

"Well, you surely got a funny way of showing it." Lon tried again to free himself. He growled at the failure. "You going to just stand there, or you going to turn me loose here?"

Her face turned dead serious as she straightened up. "Only if you make me a promise."

"Promise... promise what?"

"To help me."

Lon paused for a second to take this all in. "Now, let me get this straight. You knock me down, you tie me up, and you 'spect me to help you? Help you do what?"

"Get my papa back home."

Lon shook his head again, still not sure he understood all this. But now he was interested, even intrigued. "Where'd your papa get to?"

"He's at that tent, the gambling tent."

"Gambling tent...." He repeated it because he was uncertain he'd heard it correctly. "Look, little girl, you better start explaining proper-like you want my help."

She took in a deep breath. "I'm Marcy Lackamore. I live here with my papa, Vernon Lackamore. Early yesterday morning, my papa went to the gambling tent to try to win enough money to pay our taxes and keep the farm going till harvest when we can sell our crop. He said he'd be back last night, but he didn't come back. I'm afraid something terrible happened to him. What's your name, mister?"

Coming on the tail end of the girl's breathless statement, the question caught Lon off guard. Determined to keep his true identity hidden, he spoke as he thought, tripping a little. "It's... eh... Shawnee. Just call me Shawnee. Your papa's likely caught up in a game is all. I hear them games can go on and on for quite a spell."

"No, Papa promised me, and he always keeps his promises."

"Marcy, where's your ma?"

"Mama died these three years back."

The tears streaming down the girl's cheeks brought Lon visions of her being orphaned, and he suddenly felt almost duty bound to help her. "I'm surely sorry to hear of your loss. Look, Marcy, you let me loose, I promise I'll help you."

Marcy swiped the back of her hand over her eyes and down her cheeks as he spoke. Then she managed a smile. "I knew you would." She crouched and reached for the ropes on his wrists as he turned his body to make them accessible. Quickly she untied the knots and pulled the rope away.

As she worked, he made the decision to bid goodbye to Lon Pearce. He'd left Lon's life and identity back in Shawneetown. If he was to survive, he needed to become someone else–Shawnee. And now was as good a time as any. He sat up and rubbed his wrists where the ropes had left impressions. Then he pulled his feet under him and stood up. "Now, whereabouts is this here gambling tent?"

SHAWNEE RODE IN THE DIRECTION Marcy pointed toward. He had asked for a description of her father. She told him he was a tall, thin man in a black frock coat. As he rode, he questioned himself regarding the reasons behind his seemingly unwise decision to help this child, to get involved in a situation he had no business meddling into. The response he came up with was his original vision of her being orphaned if her father did not return. He saw her turning into him and resolved to do everything he could to prevent the loss. How he would do it was the problem he could not, at this point, figure out. All he could think of right now was to go in as quietly as possible and assess the situation before making a move. The rest he would deal with as it happened, trusting his instincts and the lessons Toby Joe taught him. Ignoring the trepidation in the back of his mind, he followed the route Marcy had indicated.

Finding the girl's directions accurate, he covered the few miles of flat Kansas plains quickly, soon coming upon the objective, a huge canvas tent the size of a small barn. It was set in the middle of an open area and was propped with supporting ropes pegged into the ground at strategic points to prevent the winds from taking it down. A picket line strung between two stout trees held a half dozen horses in check. Several buckboards in varying degrees of repair were parked near the picket. There was a sign outside, but Shawnee was still too far away to read it. A fleeting thought saying he was glad he had paid attention to his mother when she taught him to read passed as quickly as it cropped up. He kept riding until he came close enough to make out the markings and then stopped to read. Games of Chance, it stated. Shawnee touched his heels to his mount's flanks and continued to the picket line.

He pulled up and dismounted next to an attractive steel gray stallion standing proudly at about fifteen hands high. It bore a finely tooled saddle and a stout breast collar. Both horse and rigging looked expensive. His meager funds wouldn't allow it, but he'd surely admire to own them. He stared for a long moment, wondering who the owner might be, and then tied his own horse off on the line.

As he moved away from the horses, he heard the sounds of muffled conversation coming from inside the tent. It became louder as he approached the entrance, a flap opening a little taller than an average man. It rippled in the breeze but seemed to be heavy enough to remain closed in spite of the efforts of the wind. Shawnee stepped through and into a world he had never seen before.

There were round card tables and long rectangular gaming tables indiscriminately placed throughout the interior. Most of them were occupied by men of all descriptions. They were engaged in card games or were occupied at the long tables in activities which Shawnee could not identify. He had heard the terms faro and roulette, but he had never observed them and, while assuming these were what was going on, he could not tell the difference between them. Coal oil lamps, strategically placed, provided dim light to replace the daylight shut out by the heavy tenting fabric.

Shawnee moved slowly through the place, trying to keep from standing out or calling attention to himself. He gave the appearance of examining the games to decide which he would join, but, in fact, he was carefully observing each participant to locate Marcy's father. His ruse was short-lived.

As he approached and then lingered at a poker table in the center of the space, a heavy set individual in a soiled white shirt and a red brocade vest raised his head from the play. "You want something, kid?" The man's voice was smooth and smoky, seemingly a match to his pudgy stubble filled face and pencil-thin mustache. Shawnee stopped, uncertain of his next action. He thought quickly and decided to be honest. "I'm looking for a man."

"They's plenty of 'em here. Young as you are, though, it's a woman you ought to be seeking." The statement elicited chuckles from the participants at the table and put Shawnee at a disadvantage.

He gave it a moment of thought. "Ain't what I'm about." As he spoke, he scanned their faces and clothes and settled on a slim, fairly clean-shaven man dressed as Marcy had described. "Sir, are you Vernon Lackamore?"

The man in the vest flashed a perturbed look. "Kid, you interrupting our game here."

Shawnee ignored this and kept his attention on Lackamore. "Mister Lackamore, I got a message from your daughter."

Before Lackamore could answer, the man in the vest stood up. "Hey, I told you you're interrupting here. Now get out, or we'll throw you out."

Shawnee brought his hands up, palms out. "I don't want no trouble, mister." He felt a chill run up his spine at the thought of multiple men manhandling him. "Just delivering a message is all."

"Give me a minute, Bert." Lackamore's voice was calm. "Let me talk to him outside."

Bert thought for a second. "Well, all right, but you get your ass back here right quick. We got business to finish here."

Lackamore nodded and scooped up his winnings. He got up to join Shawnee. Together they moved toward the opening and went out.

Shawnee kept his voice low. "Who is that jasper?"

"Bert Ostro. He runs the place. Doing pretty well, I'd say. His gray's there on the picket. Not a cheap mount."

Shawnee nodded, taking in the proud stance and unusual color of the animal. They stopped a few steps from the flap.

"How do you know Marcy? What's her message?"

"Mister Lackamore, your daughter dropped a hay bale on me and hogtied me to get me to help her. She's worried after you. Wants you to come on home."

Lackamore chuckled. "Yeah, sounds like Marcy. Sorry she did that to you. She didn't hurt you none, did she?"

Shawnee shook his head. "No, sir."

"Will you go back to her and tell her I'm all right, and I'll be home when I win what I need to keep us going?"

"Begging your pardon, sir, but that Ostro fellow, he don't appear like he'll take too kindly to you winning on him."

"Oh, he's all right. Kind of rough around the edges, but I'm up five hundred on him, and he keeps on playing."

Shawnee was surprised at how gullible Lackamore seemed. "I reckon he'll play till he wins it back. Look, how much more you need to keep you going?"

Lackamore shrugged. "Another hundred, I guess."

"You know, Marcy, she's real concerned about you. She thinks you might lose everything. Would you consider stopping now and going home to her? I'll ride with you if you like."

"Kid, the only riding you're going to do is alone and now." Ostro's voice interrupted ominously. "Get on your animal and get the hell gone. Vern, you get back inside. We got playing to do." Ostro stood in the flap opening with a small revolver in his hand.

Shawnee turned to face the gambler. He reckoned he was right about this jasper. Toby Joe's assessment saying most people who point a gun at a body are not really ready to use it came to mind. Sometimes it was possible to face them down even though they had the drop on you.

Lackamore intervened. "Now, wait a minute, Bert. He just came to deliver a message. There's no need to order him around like that."

"I'll give the orders I want in my own place." Ostro directed his attention to Lackamore. "Now, he leaves, and you get on back inside."

Shawnee took advantage of the fleeting chance this gave him. He reached and pulled the Colt from its holster, leveling it on Ostro. "Put up that pistol, mister. I ain't fooling."

Silent, Ostro stood his ground for a moment. Shawnee watched him, watched his eyes, as Toby Joe had instructed. The man's resolve wavered. Shawnee had command of the situation. "Drop it." Ostro did it. "Mister Lackamore," Shawnee kept his attention full on Ostro. "I'm riding out. You ready to go home?"

"Well, I guess I can't have you go this far for Marcy and not go with you. Yeah, I'm ready."

"My horse is the last one on the string. Would you mind getting both yours and mine?"

Lackamore moved quickly, taking the reins of both horses and leading the animals away from the picket line. Shawnee stepped backwards toward Lackamore's location, keeping his eyes on Ostro as he moved. He would have to shift his attention away in order to mount, a chance he would have to take. He turned toward the horse as he holstered his weapon.

Faster than he ought to be, Ostro made a dive for his gun and came up firing a shot at them. The horses bolted as the ball whizzed past them, leaving Shawnee and Lackamore in the open. Recovering quickly, Shawnee grabbed Lackamore by the coat and dragged him behind the tree supporting the picket line. They reached it as Ostro sent another shot into the tree. The other horses on the line reacted. Whinnying and rearing, they yanked the rope free and created confusion in front of Ostro.

Shawnee shot a glance at Lackamore as they crouched behind the tree. "You armed?"

"Yeah."

"Well, you best get it out." Shawnee lifted his Colt out. "We're in for it now." As he contemplated his fate in the first firefight he'd ever engaged in, his mind drifted back to when this all began....

2

I T WAS AS PLAIN AS day in his memory. It hadn't been so long ago. They'd been in the field, him and his pa, for a good part of the day. He'd glanced off into the distance as he'd stopped to wipe sweat from his brow.

That's when he saw it....

"Pa, look, over there. Something's burning." He pointed in the direction of a huge plume of gray and black smoke rising in the distance. One view told him it was an active fire, and it was immense. On the Kansas plains in the summer of 1863, this day was hot. Above the billowing column, the sky was clear and blue. Strangely, the usually potent Kansas winds had abated this day, allowing the smoke to remain intact over the area in which the fire was centered.

Seth Pearce had his hands on the plow while the reins of the horse were across his shoulders and draped down his back. His call stopped the animal. He glanced over his shoulder in the direction his son indicated and took in the sight, identifying the probable location of the disturbance. "My God, that's got to be Shawneetown. Again."

Father and son stared at the event for a few seconds as memories of a similar sight returned to them from roughly a year before. It was then Quantrill and his raiders looted the tiny settlement, killed two residents, and burned the twenty-odd building community to the ground. Was the same thing happening again? Had Quantrill returned?

"You sure it's the town, Pa?"

"Too much smoke to be any of the farms 'tween here and there, and it ain't moving, so it ain't a prairie fire. I'd say the town's a safe bet."

"We should go. Maybe we can help."

"No, son. Time we got there, it'd be like last year, just a pile of smoke and rubble. Let's get back to work."

His continued stare at the smoke was cut off abruptly.

"Lon, let's get to it."

He didn't reply. He reached into the canvas sack slung across his body for a handful of seeds and deposited them into the freshly plowed furrow. His father called out to the horse, and the work continued.

They were very similar, the sixteen-year-old boy and his father of forty-two. The boy'd been christened Alonso but was called Lon. His father was Seth. Both had black, curly hair, although Seth's was now showing streaks of gray. Lon, still growing, was half a head shorter than Seth and not as well developed, but he had the potential to be a strapping man. Their faces displayed the relationship, long and lean with prominent chins and high cheekbones. The mannerisms of the pair were alike as well, the way they adjusted their wide brimmed hats and the way they moved, proudly and confidently. They had set out that morning to finish turning and planting this portion of the farm, and they were determined to complete the task. Stopping only for water and to wipe the sweat from their faces, they pushed on.

At the approach of dusk, Seth scanned across the field, content they had finished the job. "We done good work, Lon. One pasture left and the planting's done. Let's head home for supper." They collected the horse and started back to the farmhouse.

It was almost dusk, the approximate time Seth had told her in the morning to expect their return from work. As they approached the small, cabin-type farmhouse, the figure of a woman stood on the plank wood porch appearing to look out in their direction. That'd be Ma, Lon's mother, Isabel.

A small, strong bodied woman with a round, pleasant face and honey colored hair, Isabel had been married to Seth for eighteen years and was four years his senior. It had been an arranged marriage by the families, but there had always been feelings between the two. They had known each other since childhood. Matrimony seemed to be a natural next step in their relationship, but it took the relatives' urgings to bring it to fruition. Neither took the initiative, so it was taken for them.

She smiled when they'd narrowed the distance and she could positively identify them, likely content they were safe and would be with her directly. Then she turned and went back inside.

A short time later, Seth and Lon arrived, tired from the hard day. The lack of wind had made it much less difficult to direct the seeding where they wanted it, but it also provided no breeze to allay the heat of the day. Combined with backbreaking work, the intense high temperatures drained and exhausted them.

Lon put up the plow horse with a silent promise of care to be provided after supper while his father washed up near the house. He joined his father, and, as he toweled away the water dripping from his face, he glanced to the east. The column of smoke still billowed. Some dissipation had occurred since the first sighting, but it obviously still consumed fuel. Lon wondered if anyone had been hurt, or maybe killed, because of it. And he wondered if it was Quantrill at the bottom of it, like last year.

As they entered, Isabel turned from the cook stove on the far side of the combined kitchen, dining room, parlor which was the main section of the Pearce home. "Seth, I swear you two look plumb wore out."

"Dead calm out there today, Izzy, not even a bit of a breeze. We melted for sure."

"Well, you come sit down. Supper's about ready."

They pulled chairs out from the small table adjacent to the stove and sat heavily.

"Pa, better get out here. We got riders coming."

Dust rose in the distance as the horsemen drew closer. They rode at a lope, grouped tightly together. In front of the pack, a slim figure in a gray tunic and slouch hat cut a fine figure, leading proudly. This man's features were not visible to Lon until the riders were within shouting range. He was thin of face, almost gaunt, with piercing light eyes, a long neck, and narrow shoulders. His clothes were a mixture of a Confederate officer's uniform, the tunic and hat, with trousers and boots decidedly not military issue. The half dozen men who made up the complement behind him were a motley dressed crew in need of bathing and grooming. None wore any semblance of military clothing, save for the occasional Confederate kepi headgear.

As Seth joined his son on the porch, Lon discerned insignia on the officer's shoulders and hat but was at a loss for their meaning other than these were an expression of the man's rank. With his father at his side, Lon watched as the officer raised his hand to halt the group and then pulled his mount to a stop. Neither said a word.

The officer dismounted and took a step closer. "Good day to you, gentlemen. Don't be alarmed. My men and I mean you no harm." The impression he gave was of a well-spoken, articulate man, unlike the ominous appearance of his followers.

Still Seth and Lon remained quiet.

"I am Captain William Clarke Quantrill, at your service."

A slight smile crossed Seth's face. "I thought as much."

"Does my reputation precede me?"

Seth pointed to the smoke in the distance. "When I seen the smoke there, I kind of figured you was in the area. Been hearing a lot of things about you and yours of late."

Quantrill chuckled. "We do what we can to help the cause. We got word Shawnee was giving aid and comfort to the enemy by storing arms and munitions for Union forces operating in the region. They will not be doing that again anytime soon."

Lon was put off at the prospect of a mass slaying. "You kill them all?"

Seth reacted unfavorably to his son's lapse in judgment, immediately swatting the boy across his arm. "Alonso, I learned you better than to sass your elders. Now you apologize to Captain Quantrill."

Quantrill raised his hand. "Please. Do not stifle his curiosity, sir. He asks a valid question. Yes, boy, we cut down every Northern sympathizer in Shawneetown who opposed us. And we confiscated all the arms and ammunition they had. Then we burned the place, as a message to all who would engage in such endeavors. Such is the fate awaiting any who act against the Confederacy. Did I answer your question, boy?"

Lon stared at the man for a second before giving his nervous reply. "Y-Yes, sir." At least he wasn't forced to apologize.

"I take it neither of you leans toward the North."

Seth shook his head. "We just simple farmers, Captain, don't seek out no conflict. But we done seen the bluecoats in Shawneetown and how they act, all holier-'n-thou and lording over everything. Ain't no way we go along with them ways."

Quantrill smiled. "I know exactly what you mean, sir. The North's high and mighty attitude convinced me to join the Confederacy. It is for that exact reason we do what we do, to help folks like you survive."

"We appreciate it, Captain, we do for a fact. But, Lordy, where's my manners? I'm Seth Pearce and this be my son, Alonso, here. We were just about to sit down to supper. Would you care to join us?"

Quantrill stepped close enough to shake hands with Seth. "Why, I'd be pleased to sup with you, Mister Pearce. Would you mind if my men feed and water their horses? And, if you can spare some bits of food for them, I and they would greatly appreciate it."

"I'm proud to offer what little we have, Captain. It's the least we can do. Lon, you tell your mother we have company for dinner, important company."

"Yes, sir." Lon wheeled around and stepped inside the house, hearing his father continue to speak.

"You men'll find everything you need in the barn." Seth directed his attention to Quantrill. "We ain't got hardly enough room to sit all your men down inside, but we'll surely figure out a way to get them all fed. Won't you come on inside?"

"Thank you, Mister Pearce, I'd be delighted."

Seth opened the house door and escorted Quantrill inside. Quantrill removed his hat as Isabel turned from the stove to face them, a platter of fried chicken in her hands.

"Isabel, this is Captain Quantrill, come to call. Captain, this is my wife, Isabel."

"Welcome to our home." Isabel's smile was welcoming, but her eyes said something else. She allowed Lon to take the platter from her.

"A pleasure, ma'am." Quantrill bowed with flourish. "I thank you for your hospitality."

"Please have a seat." Isabel gestured to the table. As Quantrill bowed slightly and stepped past her, the smile she had forced herself to wear in his presence left her face. The frown she flashed at Seth told a different story.

Isabel and Lon brought the food to the table and everyone sat down, Quantrill making a point of pulling the chair out for Isabel. Seth and Quantrill carried on a spirited conversation while Isabel and Lon remained quiet. Besides Quantrill complimenting Isabel's cooking, the talk ranged from Quantrill's early life as a teacher to his enlistment in the Confederate Army to his current undertaking, the searching out and destruction of the hated Yankee invaders. He explained that this encompassed military expeditionary forces as well as civilian Northern sympathizers known as Jayhawkers, who operated out of Shawneetown and Lawrence as well as several points in Western Missouri. "It's a thankless job, but one for which my force is uniquely qualified. We're called Bushwhackers for a reason." His tone of voice changed from conversational to oratorical. "I took poor farmers, some of whom were turned into outlaws because of their beliefs, and whipped them into a fierce fighting unit able to beat the bushes for Northern soldiers and Jayhawkers. Using the tactics I taught them, they frequently prevail over superior odds."

Seth listened intently to the tales Quantrill told, showing more interest in them than Lon had ever seen in his father. As well, he saw the distaste in his mother's expressions, reading her intolerance of this man who thought more of himself than was actually there.

"You would be helping to secure your farm from being ripped from you by the Yankee invaders," Quantrill told Seth. He made other similar comments during the conversation, and, each time, Lon observed Seth falling further under the man's spell.

When the meal ended, Quantrill rose and thanked Isabel for providing the best meal he had had "in a month of Sundays." He turned to Seth. "I have a couple of good cigars here. Would you care to retire to the porch? We can continue to converse."

"Don't mind if I do."

The two went outside into the cool night and sat on the porch steps.

As they lit up, Lon picked up a tray of food, stopping just inside the doorway. Mesmerized by his father's enchantment with Quantrill, he listened.

"One thing's eating at me, Captain. I'd have thought you'd have a heap more men than half a dozen coming off the Shawnee raid."

"I do. I split the force when we left Shawnee. We scattered in all directions. Tactics such as these not only allow us to attack and defeat the enemy but to confuse and confound them as well."

Seth nodded. While he and his guest enjoyed their cigars, Quantrill assured Seth he was an excellent candidate to join the Bushwhackers. Flattered, Seth expressed his desire to protect his family and property and to help secure a Confederate victory.

"You know, by joining me, Seth, you can contribute to both those lofty aspirations."

As much as Seth wanted to join Quantrill's band, he had one firm condition. "It'd be only me coming. I need Lon to stay and work the farm. 'Sides, I'd never put him in danger."

"Of course. He is your son. You have the say in his future."

"I ain't never done nothing like this before. Don't know how I'd fare in a fight."

"I'll put you with two of my best men. They'll help you. We take care of our own. You'll see."

"I reckon so." They shook hands on the bargain.

"If you don't mind, we'll stay the night in the barn, and you can leave with us in the morning."

"Sure thing."

Standing there flatfooted, Lon came back to reality as Seth and Quantrill got up from the porch. The conversation was over, and he needed to get back to what he'd intended to do. He stepped out and walked quickly past them toward the barn.

It was later that night when Lon and Isabel received the news from Seth of his decision. Isabel was shocked, Lon less so because of his eavesdropping. Isabel put her reaction into loudly spoken words. "Seth, have you lost your mind? What those men do is dangerous, and I'm not all that sure it's right."

Lon stood trancelike, riveted by the most heated exchange he'd ever seen between his parents.

"You heard what Captain Quantrill said, Izzy. The Yankees is trying to take over everything. Him and his Bushwhackers, they's trying to keep 'em out. If I don't do something to help them, we'll be all alone when them Yankees show up here, and we won't have a chance. I got to do this. It's to protect the family."

Isabel turned her back on her husband. "Seth, this is wrong. Your place is here with us. That man is not what you think he is, what he says he is. He's leading you on with his stories and his fancy words. I'll tell you what he is. He's an opportunist. Why is he leading such a scruffy bunch? Why aren't they in uniform? He's just like them, a ruffian, out for whatever he can get from whoever he can get it from. And he'll turn you into one of them as well."

"It ain't like that, Izzy. This ain't like the real war back east. Back there, they got armies and all. Out here, it's every man for himself, unless we all band together. We got to help each other, or we'll all die alone."

Isabel turned to face him. Tears ran down her cheeks. Her fists were clenched at her sides. "He's not helping you. Can't you see? He's helping himself. He's building his force. What does he care he's taking you away from your responsibilities, your family? It's hard enough for the three of us to keep this place up. Now you're leaving it to Lon and me? Don't do this, Seth. Tell him no."

"No, I can't. I won't. I already give my word, and I ain't going back on it. I'm leaving with Captain Quantrill in the morning, and that's the all and done of it. I'll say no more on it."

Isabel took in a deep breath to deliver her next words. "What you're doing is foolish and irresponsible. If you go, you go without my blessing."

Seth nodded once. "So be it." He turned sharply and left the house.

Isabel broke down in tears as Lon wrapped his arms around her to console his mother. When she recovered slightly, Isabel forced out, "Don't you even think about going with him, young man."

"No, Ma, I ain't." Lon said that with all the conviction he could muster.

3

A ROOSTER CROWED TO ANNOUNCE the arrival of dawn. Lon rolled out from a restless night, having been unable to calm his mind enough to allow sleep to take him over. He assumed his mother was still in her room, not seeing her anywhere in the cabin. His father had retreated the night before, after the argument with her, to the barn to sleep with Quantrill and his men, electing to allay any further exchange. Lon dressed quickly and quietly and stepped out onto the porch as the barn door came open to allow the exit of a stream of men leading saddled horses. Among them, he saw his father and Quantrill.

"Time we got moving," Quantrill said as the raiders mounted.

His weapons and possessions with him, Seth mounted his horse wearily. Lon guessed his father'd had the same kind of night as he had.

Quantrill addressed Seth as he mounted. "You'd best say your goodbyes. No telling when we'll be back this way."

"I said all I had to say last night. It didn't go down easy, so I'll say no more. Maybe someday she'll understand what I'm doing is right, but it ain't going to be this day."

"I'm sorry it went that way, Seth. Womenfolk don't seem to understand these ways."

Seth nodded.

Apprehensive, Lon went directly to his father. Seth leaned over in the saddle to hear his son's words.

"Pa, you be careful and come back to us."

"I'll be fine, son. These is good men I got around me. We'll look out each for the other. I can feel it. You take good care of your ma and you. Get hold of Toby Joe you need help, you hear?"

"Yes, Pa, I will."

Seth's hand reached out and wrapped itself around Lon's neck in a loving gesture.

"Let's ride." Quantrill's voice was loud as he urged his horse forward. The men, including Seth, fell in behind and followed.

Lon stood in the center of the yard, watching the group ride away. The impression of his father's strong hand on the back of his neck still remained. His hand went to that position as if to touch Seth's hand, not knowing when he would feel the touch again. He stood there holding his neck until the raiders were but a dot on the horizon.

"Lon." Lon turned at the sound. It came from the porch. Isabel stood just outside the door in her night clothes. "Yes, Ma?"

"Come inside. It'll do you no good watching after them. They're gone and him with them."

Lon went quickly to his mother.

"It's good you saw your father before he left. It's likely the last time you'll see him."

"Aw, Ma, don't say that. You don't know it for a fact."

"There's a feeling I got, a deep down feeling. He won't be coming back. You might as well get used to it. Now come inside. We got work to do."

———

ᵎ OUT OF THE barn, brushing hay from his clothing.

ᵎ, he glanced in the direction of Shawneetown to see ɪɪ traces oɪ the previous day's fire were still evident. No smoke was visible, but his gaze did pick up a group of riders approaching from the town's general location. The Kansas wind was beginning to return. It carried away any dust kicked up by the horsemen before it could be seen from a distance, thus the group was able to draw closer before being noticed. Uncertain of their identity, Lon hurried to the house porch and leaned past the partially open door. "Ma, we got more riders coming."

Isabel turned from the stove. "Can you tell who they are?"

"They ain't close enough yet, but they're headed in from Shawnee-way."

Isabel joined Lon on the porch, and both strained their vision to make out who this group might be. Distance forced them to wait until the riders came closer, but then Isabel spoke up. "I can make out Mister Teverence there."

"Yeah, and I see Old Sam, the tracker fellow. They likely trying to run the Bushwhackers down."

Isabel nodded. "They'll be looking for your father to join them."

Lon realized Seth's absence would cause suspicion, or at least a question. He put his mind to work quickly. "Let me talk to them, Ma."

They stood on the porch as the group rode up and stopped behind Teverence. He was medium in height and substantially broad even though he was not physically well developed. Long and lean, his face was pleasant and was framed with well-groomed light brown hair. Reflecting his higher station, his clothes were expensive and well tailored. They did now seem unkempt after going through the rigors of a firefight and the ensuing bucket brigade which must have unsuccessfully attempted to extinguish multiple blazes through the twenty or so buildings making up the town. He leaned forward and propped his forearm on the pommel of his saddle. "How do, Miz Pearce, Lon."

"Mister Teverence." Isabel spoke quietly, not very accepting.

Lon simply nodded.

"You likely seen the smoke yesterday. That blackguard, Quantrill, and his Bushwhackers, they burned the town... again. Killed a lot of good folks this time. We'd have been closer on 'em, but it took us a time to fight the fires and care for the wounded. But we out to get 'em now. You ain't seen 'em, have you?"

"Yes, sir, we did," Lon shuffled for a second as he thought. "They... eh... they stopped here yesterday near sundown. Asked to water their horses. We was scared not to, so we let them."

"Reckon you done the safe thing. No telling what they'd a did if'n you folks said no. Say, where's your pa? He about?"

"No, sir. He... headed up to Kansas City yesterday."

"Kansas City? What's up there?"

"We busted our plow yesterday. He would have went to Shawnee-town for a new one, but we done seen the smoke coming from that-a-way. He reckoned it wouldn't do no good going there, so he headed out for Kansas City right off."

Teverence straightened in his saddle. "Well, now, you surely got a bad break right in the middle of planting season, didn't you?"

"Yes, sir, and us having a whole pasture left undone."

"Long way to go for a plow. Reckon he done right though."

"Yes, sir."

Teverence let out a loud sigh. "I was going to ask Seth to join us, but, since he ain't here.... Say, what about you, Lon? You can ride with us."

"No." Isabel was sharp and definite. "No, I need Lon here."

Teverence pursed his lips, showing his disappointment. "Yeah, reckon you're right, ma'am. It's all right. We can handle it. Reckon we'll be getting on now. You folks have a good day." He pulled his reins and set out, leading the group west at a lope.

As they passed, Lon and his mother turned to watch them ride off.

"Alonzo Pearce!" Isabel smacked Lon's arm. "Where did you learn to bend the truth like you just did?" Her voice was harsh, scolding him.

"I surely don't know, Ma. It just come upon me."

"See you learn to control your lying, young man. If I didn't agree with what you did, I'd be washing your mouth out with soap about now. You're not too old for that, you know."

Lon smiled slightly. "Yes, Ma."

4

DAYS FADED INTO EACH OTHER as Lon took on the job of two men, working alone in the fields while Isabel continued to take care of her normal duties and helped Lon where she could. Before they knew it, two weeks had passed with no word from Seth.

As darkness settled in on the fourteenth day, Lon, inside the cabin with Isabel, responded to a thump just outside. Before him, a riderless, unsaddled horse stood beside the collapsed figure of a man. Lon approached. He looked up as Lon came close, allowing Lon to recognize him in the light glimmering from inside the house.

"Pa!"

Seth responded with a wan smile and attempted to get to his feet. His effort resulted in failure, putting him down on all fours. Lon went to his side and helped him up.

"Pa, what happened? You hurt?"

Seth could not speak. As he regained his feet, Isabel appeared in the doorway. "Oh, God. Seth!" She assisted Lon to take Seth inside. By the time they hauled him to the bed, exhaustion had overtaken him. He lost consciousness.

Several days passed during which Seth drifted in and out of consciousness. Isabel tried with some success to get food into him. It was mostly broths at first, then he was able to consume light meals. Gradually, his strength and lucidity began returning. In bits and pieces, he related the ordeal he'd gone through after joining the Bushwhackers. His first taste of battle, an attack on a wagon train of supplies and munitions bound for Lawrence, Kansas, to be distributed to Union forces, resulted in a total massacre of the Union guards and the men tending the wagons. The only one Seth knew to have escaped was the driver of the lead wagon who sprinted into the woods when Seth failed to kill him. The entire incident turned him against Quantrill's mission, but his request of the captain to be released from his commitment so he could return home was denied. He was put in irons and forced to work with the cook crew until he and a fellow prisoner overpowered the cook and skedaddled. He had no idea how long it took him to reach home. All he knew was he had to keep going.

"Did they come after you, Pa? You seen a lot of what they done. Maybe we should ought to be ready, case they show up."

"I kept on sighting back, son. Never seen a one of 'em. Way I cipher it, Quantrill believes he's in the right, and he don't care who knows what he done. Reckon he wants it knowed. It adds to his reputation and scares folks."

Lon shook his head. "He surely ain't what he thinks he is."

"Yeah, I know that now."

"I honestly thought I'd never see you again." Isabel sounded relieved. "It's good you're home."

Several days of rest, good food, and loving care put Seth on the road to recovery. Isabel devoted those days exclusively to his needs and gradually her labors bore fruit. Finally up and around, he was able to join the family one evening at the dinner table.

After washing up, Lon sat down with them.

Seth's expression was contrite. "Look, I'm sorry what I put you through. I was wrong. Reckon I got took in by Quantrill, like you said, Izzy. What I seen in the short time I's with the Bushwhackers woke me up to what they really be. You was right, Izzy, and I'm truly sorry."

Isabel took a moment to digest his words. "The important thing is you're home, and you're safe."

"Ain't real sure how safe you be, Pa." Lon showed concern. "Maybe Quantrill ain't after you, but that Teverence fellow and his bunch been snooping around here of late, ever since you went off. Keeps asking after you."

"Next time he shows up, I'll talk to him."

"It might be better if you don't," Isabel said.

"He might run the Jayhawkers and Shawneetown, but, at least, I think he's a fair man. I reckon he'll hear me out."

"I don't know, Pa. He appears bound and determined to find you. And I don't reckon it's to listen. I think he's of a mind to do you harm."

"I can't believe that of him. I don't see him as the kind who'd look to hurt a friend he's did so much for hereabouts. But, even if he is, I ain't hiding from him. Don't reckon he can put any worse to me than I already went through."

Lon and Isabel exchanged a glance, betraying their suspicions and disbelief. Seth paid it no heed. The meal proceeded without further discussion.

Early the next morning Lon went to the fields to finish the work he had been doing the day before. Seth remained at the house with Isabel. After some urging by Lon and Isabel, he agreed to get back his full strength before attempting anything physical.

Later that day, Lon looked around from his plowing. Isabel, clinging to the back of a horse with no saddle, rode flat out toward him. Her shouts and her mannerisms told him something was terribly wrong. He'd never seen his mother on a horse, much less riding flat out like she was. Immediately, he threw off the plow horse's reins and ran in her direction. Out of breath by the time they reached each other, he forced out his question as she pulled up beside him. "Ma, what's wrong?"

"They took him. They took your pa." She was frantic.

"Took him… *who* took him?"

"Jayhawkers. Teverence and some others."

"Where'd they take him?"

"I don't know. They said they knew he'd been with the Bush-whackers. Looked like they headed toward Shawneetown."

"That ain't good. Tell you what, give me your horse. You take Sandy there." He indicated the plow horse. "You go on back to the house and wait there. I'll try to pick up their trail."

As Isabel got down, Lon took the reins from her and swung up on the horse. He turned toward the house, going to an immediate gallop. Pushing the animal for everything it was worth, he rode into the yard and pulled up sharply. A quick scan of the earth in front of the house showed him fresh tracks. His eyes followed them as they turned and rode away. With very limited tracking abilities, it was difficult to count the amount of horses involved, but they were visible enough and fresh enough for him to stay on them. He moved out, going as fast as he could without losing the trail, noting the group had veered away from the route to Shawneetown as soon as they cleared the main farm area.

After tracking the group for several minutes, he found himself approaching a stand of red oak trees. There was movement in the distance. Convinced he had come upon the Jayhawkers who had taken his father, he abandoned the trail and set out straight for them with no plan of what he would do when he reached them. As he gained ground, he saw them examining several trees. One man had dismounted. The man slung a rope over different limbs and suspended himself on the end to test the strength of each bough. They were fixing to hang Pa. It echoed in his head as he kicked his heels into the horse's flanks to generate more speed. Still, he had no idea how to handle this except to ride into them and attempt to disrupt them. Maybe, in the confusion, he could get to his father and the two could escape.

As he drew near, the man with the rope selected a suitable branch and remounted. Lon kept going. He spotted Seth in the middle of the group as Teverence and Daylock, the hardware storekeeper, saw Lon coming. Then Seth saw him. "Lon, no!"

Lon slammed his heels harder into his mount. The group turned to move into a barrier between Seth and the oncoming Lon, but Lon ignored the obstruction. He was at top speed when he crashed his horse into the group. Mass confusion combined with terrified equine whinnies and human cries as horses and men spilled over onto the ground.

Lon's horse was one of the fallen, but Lon was lucky enough to be thrown clear to land on his side. Some of the Jayhawkers were pinned under their mounts while others were able to remain in their saddles. Two who were not affected were Teverence and Daylock. Lon saw Teverence go directly to Seth to grab his reins and cover him with his handgun. Daylock dismounted close to where Lon had landed.

Slightly stunned, Lon rolled from his back to his knees in an attempt to get up. Daylock reached him while he was still on his hands and knees and swung a kick at his head. The side of the boot connected with Lon's forehead and sent him to the ground on his back. Pain from the blow filled his head. Now further dazed, Lon still attempted to regain his feet. Daylock stepped in and hit him as he was rising, catching him across the jaw and spinning him around. More pain came, but somehow, Lon remained standing. Daylock attacked again with a belly blow and uppercut, putting Lon out of the fight. He dropped heavily to the ground with unintelligible shouts sounding around him, and, as he drifted into unconsciousness, the last thing he saw was his father, still mounted, being led to a position under the waiting rope.

5

"LON... ALONSO."

The call was distant. The jostling accompanying it could hardly be perceived. Slowly, Lon's senses awoke. What had happened? Oh, yeah. It started coming back a little, then in a rush. Pa, they were hanging Pa. He tried to focus his eyes, but all he saw was... was that a shirt? Yeah, a shirt. It was kind of familiar. The voice calling his name again was familiar as well. Toby Joe? What the hell—

The figure in the shirt shifted a little, allowing Lon to see beyond it.

"Pa! No!" Lon shouted as the scene before him confirmed the condition of his father. Lon lifted himself on elbows to improve his view. Seth dangled there, several feet off the ground, hands bound behind his back, a rope tight around his neck, his head in an awkward angle, mouth wide open. They done it. They hung him.

Lon fell back into a crumble of grief. "No, no, no, no."

The voice above him offered consolation. "I'm sorry, Lon. Wished I got here soon enough to stop this." It was Toby Joe Hawks, all right, no doubt about his voice.

Lon did not reply but continued to fall further into anguish. Hawks forced his body to maintain the uncomfortable position blocking Lon's view until Lon was able to regain himself and calm down some.

When he deemed it prudent, Hawks relaxed and allowed himself to roll to a seat beside Lon. Lon stared at his father's body. Hawks placed a comforting hand on Lon's shoulder. "Don't be looking there, boy. It'll do you no good."

"I tried to stop them." Lon's murmur was hardly audible.

"I know. Nothing you could a did. I know you tried your best."

Lon now became more rational, and his speech became more understandable. "This ain't right. They hung him without a trial. They're supposed to have a trial and let folks have they's say. But they just strung him up, and now he's dead."

"I know, Lon. Ain't none of this right, none of it. But, look-a-here, boy, we got to do for your pappy. Sure as hell can't leave him up there. We got to get him down, take him home, bury him proper-like. I can't do it by my lonesome, boy. You up to helping me?"

Lon regarded Hawks, his first time taking his eyes off Seth. A short man with a game leg, the result of a horse fall several years back, Hawks was just shy of fifty-years-old with a round face and broad shoulders. He wore suspender braced trousers and a Henley-type long sleeve shirt with a wide brimmed straw hat and knee length boots worn outside the pant legs. His injury caused his leg to straighten permanently. He'd been neighbor and friend to the Pearce family for longer back than Lon could recollect. It was good he was here.

Lon's, "I reckon," was uncertain at best. He swept the tears from his eyes and face with the back of his hand.

Hawks stared him squarely in the eye. "This is likely the hardest thing you'll ever have to do, but it's got to be did. You set there a spell. I'll see if I can figure a way we can get 'er done." He scrambled to his feet, the stiff leg an encumbrance, and studied the problem. "You got a horse?"

Lon glimpsed around. "Somewheres hereabouts, I reckon."

Hawks walked the area and, after a few minutes, found the animal grazing a few yards away. He led the horse back to where Lon was now up on shaky legs. "What I'm thinking is, one of us holds the horse next to your pappy and the other one looses the rope. Then we can sling Seth across the horse. Question is, which one you up to doing?"

Lon thought for a second. "The rope. I'll work the rope."

Hawks nodded and placed the horse beside Seth's body. Then he mounted his own animal and moved to a spot on the other side of the body. While this went on, Lon went to the tree trunk at which the rope end was tied off. Hawks called to him. "Loose it. And ease it down." Lon followed the instructions, forcing his body to put out the strength to support the weight of his father's body. Hawks gently guided the corpse across the back of the waiting horse until Seth was in position face down.

Lon hurried to the animal's side and somehow found the inner strength to remove the noose from Seth's neck. He took the blanket roll from Hawks's saddle and gently tucked it around the body as a shroud.

Hawks pulled a foot from the stirrup. "Get up here behind me, boy. We'll take Seth home."

———————————

THEY MOVED SLOWLY, LON AND Hawks riding double with Lon leading the horse carrying the body of his father. Isabel, obviously distraught, stood clinging to a porch post outside the house as they moved toward her. She seemed like she could barely stay upright. She appeared to be shuddering, perhaps weeping.

Lon wanted desperately to get to his mother, to console, to comfort her, but they couldn't hurry. It surely wouldn't do for Seth's body to be jostled off a horse moving too fast. It was terrible now, but that would only make it worse.

Hawks finally drew rein at the porch as Isabel gazed up at them, seemingly aware of the situation but trying not to be. Lon quickly put a foot in the left stirrup and swung down. Isabel sagged and slid down the pillar into a clump on the porch as Lon reached her. His touch was all it took to send her over the edge. Hysterics followed as Lon crouched to her level and scooped her into his arms. She gripped him and hung onto him, crying uncontrollably. He said calming things softly to her, not really aware of what he said, but she heard none of it, her cries drowning it out. They remained there for many minutes, with the still mounted Hawks looking on helplessly.

As Isabel gradually began to regain herself, Lon slowly repositioned her so Seth's body was no longer in her field of vision. Then he helped her up, supporting her, and gently moved her inside the house. He walked her to the table and pulled out one of the chairs for her to sit on. Her hands were clasped as if in prayer, and she placed the index fingers across her lips in a contemplative motion as she sniffled her way back to control. She ended up staring aimlessly straight ahead with Lon crouching beside her.

Hawks stepped through the doorway and went to Lon. He laid his hand on Lon's shoulder. Lon turned his head to him. "You stay with your ma. I'll see to what needs doing." Lon nodded and returned his attention to his mother as Hawks went outside and led the horse bearing Seth's body away.

Over time stretching into the afternoon, Lon doted on his mother, calming her, making her tea, administering to her needs. Eventually, she returned to a state of control, albeit still distraught.

During this, Hawks remained outside, laboring quietly to do what needed doing. Lon was aware of Hawks's effort and the fact his handicap made the task even more difficult, but he stayed with his mother, deeming it more important to see to her needs and to prevent her from seeing Seth's grave being dug. He was sure Hawks would understand.

"Lon," Hawks called from the doorway. Lon turned from his mother. A gesture from Hawks silently asked him to come closer. He complied. "I dug a grave for your pa," Hawks said in a whisper. "You want me to finish the burying?"

"I'll help you. Give me a minute."

Hawks stepped out. Lon returned to Isabel. "I got to help Mister Hawks for a spell, Ma. You all right?" Isabel nodded. Lon left her to join Hawks at the gravesite, several yards behind the house. Together they lifted the shrouded body from the horse and placed it gently into the opening. Lon took one last look before moving the displaced earth over his father. When he finished, Hawks stepped to his side, again placing a hand on the boy's shoulder, and both stood at the foot of the grave, contemplating their loss.

"Mister Hawks, I swear I'm going to get them that done this, ever last one of them."

"No, Lon, no." Isabel walked on unsteady legs to her son's side. "I've lost your father. I will *not* lose you, too. I forbid it."

Lon stared at the grave, attempting to ignore Isabel's statement. He would do this with or without her permission.

Isabel persisted. "Lon?"

"All right, Ma, I'll leave off." He said that just to pacify his mother.

Isabel stared at the grave. Lon felt her hand on his arm as she sagged under the strain. He grabbed her and helped her to walk back to the house.

Lon stepped out of the house at dusk. Hawks stood at the edge of the porch staring into the horizon while puffing on a corncob pipe. Lon went to Hawks's side. "She's sleeping."

"Good." Hawks spoke with teeth clamped around the pipe stem. "Reckon she'd be tuckered after all this."

"Mister Hawks—"

Hawks turned to Lon. "Lon, what you been through today, you earned the right to call me by my given name."

"Toby Joe, then, what I said to Ma, about leaving off getting the ones hung Pa, I didn't mean that. I was just trying to settle Ma down."

Hawks took the pipe out of his mouth. "I know you didn't, Lon. I know you better'n that. But, I got to tell you, you ain't got neither the learning nor the wherewithal to pull it off. You bull on into it now, you'll sure as hell get yourself killt."

"Will you help me with the learning?"

Hawks thought for a second. "I reckon so."

"But I don't want Ma to know nothing about it."

Another second of thinking passed before Hawks continued. "You come on over to my place in the morning. We'll come up with something. Come early. We got a lot to cover."

"Yes, sir, I'll be there. And thank you, for that and all you done today."

"Ain't nothing. Least I can do. Seth was a good man and a good friend. Didn't no way deserve what they done to him."

Seething, Lon sucked in a breath. "They'll pay."

Hawks put a hand on the boy's shoulder, trying to temper his rage. "Steady, son. This ain't nothing to rush into. And nothing to try at when you're riled. You'll get there, by and by."

Hawks left soon after. Lon sat quietly on the porch, reflecting on the events of the day and worrying over his mother's fragile state. She was strong, but he was uncertain how she would pull through this and what he could do to help her. He also knew the path he was preparing to go down would likely make the situation worse, but it had to be done, come what might. He sat there into the night, pondering on that.

Dawn found Lon hunkered over, his head resting on his knees. He had closed his eyes somewhere during the night, and exhaustion caused a restless doze which did little to replenish him. The emerging daylight caused his eyes to open. Immediately, he hurt in many places, the culmination of the previous day's beating and the aches of a prolonged uncomfortable position. He forced through them and got to his feet. A long stretch got the blood flowing again, and he realized where he was and what had happened. His concern instantly became his mother. Quietly, he stepped into the house to find Isabel also rising from a tense sleep.

Without a word, he went to her, sat beside her on the bed, and embraced her. They stayed there for several minutes, comforting each other.

Then Lon began the lie. "I should get out to finish the planting."

"I know." She rested a hand on his. "You wash up. I'll get breakfast started. We have to go on."

"Yes, Ma."

Lon did as he was told, marveling at the resilience his mother displayed. He picked at his food, forcing himself to eat at least a small amount to maintain his strength. Across from him at the table, he noted Isabel hardly eating as well. When the meal was finished, he went to the barn and prepared the horse to take him into the field. This was the point at which the lie manifested itself. Once out of sight of the house, he diverted to take the route to Hawks's cabin.

As Lon approached the small cottage, Hawks was out front, apparently awaiting his arrival. Freshly skinned hides hung drying on racks set up on either side of the house. Lon recalled Hawks made his living making articles out of leather. The hides were where it started.

"Morning," Hawks said as Lon pulled up and slid off.

"Morning."

"We got a lot to do, so let's get to it."

Lon followed him to a large tree stump where several articles had been laid out.

"This here's a Colt's Navy model. Shoots a thirty-six caliber ball. Accurate as hell. That'n there's a Sharp's carbine. It's for long distance shooting. Ain't neither of these loaded yet. All part of your learning. Pick 'em up. Get the heft of 'em."

Lon followed his instructor's directions carefully, first picking up and examining the revolver and then the carbine. Hawks precisely taught the handling, loading, and firing of both weapons throughout the morning. Lon was an enthusiastic and quick learner. "The carbine fires a paper 'catridge,'" Hawks displayed the ammunition and went through the motions. "That there's a fifty-two caliber round. Kicks like a mule. You drop the trigger guard, slip the 'catridge' all the way in the chamber, like this, and close 'er up. Now it's locked. You pull back the hammer, put a cap on the nipple, and you're ready to shoot." He put down the rifle and picked up the revolver. "Now the Colt's a whole different animal. Shoots a lead ball." He demonstrated the process as he described it. "You start by measuring out the powder with this here thing-a-ma-bob. You put a charge in the chamber, set a ball in place. Now this here's the ramrod. Crank down on it real hard till the ball's seated. Now this here puts a bit of grease on the chamber. There you go. Seals it and keeps the other chambers from going off when you fire that one. Hell to pay if'n you get one of them. Now you caps up the nipples and you're all set. Mind you, you only load five chambers, and you keep the hammer riding on the empty one so's it don't go off unexpected-like. Now you do it."

Lon went through the loading processes of both weapons, then he concentrated on the carbine. By the approach of the noon hour, he was proficient in loading, firing, and reloading the Sharp's.

"Let's get a bite to eat," Hawks said. "Then we'll work on the pistol."

During their brief meal, Hawks related his experiences with bands of raiders similar to Quantrill's Bushwhackers, crediting these with developing his gun handling skills. He also attributed his leg injury to them, stating the horse he was riding was shot out from under him. The fall smashed the leg, and it was never the same after. "Time to get back to work."

They spent half of the afternoon working on the revolver and the balance on accuracy training. By the end of the day, Lon was a decent shot with both weapons.

"You done fine today, Lon." Hawks led the way back to the tree stump. "Just need to keep practicing." He picked up the military style holster, from which the top flap had been cut away, and belt resting there. He handed them to Lon. "Here, try this on." Lon strapped the belt around his waist and inserted it in the loop of the holster. He stood there as Hawks adjusted the rig on Lon's hips, dropped the Colt into the holster, butt forward, and then gave him the carbine. "Them's yours now. Treat 'em right, and they'll do likewise for you."

"Aw, Toby Joe, I can't take these. You won't have nothing to defend yourself with."

"Don't you worry none about me. I got me a Henry rifle inside. Loads sixteen 'catridges.' More'n enough to keep me in hides and out of trouble."

6

AS DUSK BEGAN DISPLACING DAYLIGHT, Lon and Hawks approached the farm. "I'll hide the guns in the hayloft," Lon said as they rode. "Ma doesn't never go up there."

"You going to have to tell her sooner or later. You know that, don't you?"

"I know, but it'll be later."

They directed their horses into the yard. Lon kept his eyes on the house, making certain he would not be visible to Isabel until he had the chance to hide the weapons. His attention was repositioned when Hawks said with a start, "What the hell?" Lon focused where Hawks pointed at the form on the ground in front of the barn. He instantly realized it was his mother. Panic gripped him. "Ma!"

Dropping down from the horse, he went on a dead run to Isabel's body, letting go of the rifle on his way. He folded to his knees and rolled her on her back, revealing the wound and the blood covering a substantial portion of her face. Copious amounts of blood stained the ground around where her face and upper body had rested.

Hawks dismounted and hurried to them, but Lon paid no attention. He was locked in place by the sight of Isabel's condition. Hawks went down in his straight-legged squat and reached to Isabel's neck.

"She's dead, Lon." Lon did not move, did not hear his friend. Hawks shook Lon. "Lon, she's...." This time Lon heard, but the words did not register. He reached down and lifted Isabel's head. "Ma, wake up." He shouted frantically. "It's Lon. Wake up."

Hawks shook his head. "Ain't no use, son."

This finally got through to Lon. "No, you can't die. Don't leave me." Accompanying his cries, he shook her body in a desperate attempt to rouse her. Realizing the futility of this, he collapsed in grief, his head resting on her breast. He cried uncontrollably.

Hawks reached his hand to Lon's shoulder and squeezed it tightly, as if trying to transmit support to the boy. He remained in that position for several minutes while Lon bawled loudly.

It took a while for Lon to recover. He leaned back on his haunches, and, with tears still running down his cheeks, he looked at Hawks. "She's dead." His words matched his incredulous expression. It was almost as if Hawks was not aware of the fact.

"I know, son, I know." Hawks squeezed Lon's shoulder again.

"She can't be dead. Toby Joe, what am I going to do?"

Hawks cleared his throat to stifle an emotional catch in his voice. "You go on, Lon. All's you can do is, you go on."

Lon stared into space for a long time, collecting himself.

Hawks glanced around, more to take his mind off the incident, but his eyes came upon something on the ground next to Isabel's body. He scurried around to get a better view of the scrawl scratched into the earth. It was definitely writing, but his inability to read put him at a disadvantage. "Lon, look-a-here." He reached to touch Lon to get his attention. "What's this say?"

Lon raised his eyes to the indicated location and tried to decipher the scribble. Slowly, he realized it was likely written by his mother. "Tev... Teverence," he read aloud. It was erratically scratched, likely with the twig laying nearby, the letters not evenly spaced or sized. The end trailed off, but it positively spelled out the name. This allowed him to think, logically, if not rationally. "She wrote Teverence. Teverence done this to her. Teverence killed Ma." He turned to face Hawks. "I'm going to kill him, Toby Joe. I'm going to go to Shawneetown, and I'm going to kill him sure."

"Slow down, Lon. You ain't thinking clear. You ain't near ready for nothing like that."

"I don't care," Lon's teeth were clenched. "Teverence killed Ma and Pa. He's got to die."

Hawks turned Lon and looked him squarely in the eye. "You're right, you're right, but we got something else to do first." He motioned his head toward Isabel.

Lon took the meaning. He reluctantly got up and went into the house. Seconds later, he emerged with a blanket. Hawks took it from him and set about wrapping Isabel's body. Lon went into the barn and brought out a shovel. He walked past the scene and went to the rear of the house where his father was buried. Immediately, he began digging a second grave beside Seth's, going about this with a vengeance, betraying the wrath within him.

It was dark when Lon finished the excavation. He refused Hawks's help and pushed on until he was close to exhaustion while Hawks provided coal oil lamps for light. Together, they returned to the yard and gently lifted Isabel's remains, Lon steeling himself to carry this out without faltering. They transported her slowly to the gravesite and placed her there. Standing side by side, they clasped their hands and spent a silent moment of remembrance. Lon sniffed back a runny nose caused by the tears of his grief. He picked up the shovel, took a deep breath, and began placing earth over the body until the mound closely matched the one covering Seth.

When it was finished, Lon returned the shovel to the barn, carrying a lamp to light his way. Hawks followed with the second light. Lon left the barn and went directly to his horse, retrieving the rifle on the way.

"Lon, where you going?"

"Teverence." Lon swung up on the bareback horse.

Hawks stepped closer, taking hold of the halter at the horse's mouth. "Lon, listen to me. You got to wait till you're ready. You go now, you'll get yourself killt."

"I told you I don't care. Teverence got to die. I ain't waiting."

"Lon—"

Lon pulled the horse free and kicked his heels into its flanks to generate an immediate gallop. Hawks called out to him again as he rode off, but Lon ignored it.

SHAWNEETOWN WAS A SHAMBLES. PARTIALLY burned buildings, as well as those completely destroyed by the fire, stood beside each other. Rubble from the clean-up littered the streets. The pungent odor of charred wood emanating from the ruins hung over the location even after the Kansas winds did their best to dissipate them. Darkness and the weariness of the residents brought repairs and renovations to a halt at the end of daylight. It would start up again early the next morning once they had rested.

Into this muddle, Lon rode slowly. The sights around him did not shock him since he had seen the results of the previous raid a year earlier. It was still an upsetting scene, this mass destruction. It evoked the same reaction now as he had experienced then. This was a savage assault that went far beyond what might have been required.

He glanced around as he progressed, taking in what was visible in the darkness. Only a few lamps here and there provided a low level of light, but what he could see, combined with the persistent smells, told him the horrific story. Directing his horse toward a small group of people clustered together in conversation, he remained fixated on his objective, locating and killing Carl Teverence.

"Evening, folks." Lon dismounted near the gathering. "Can anybody tell me where I might find Carl Teverence?" He did his best to sound cordial, trying not to give away his true intention.

The group turned their attention to Lon as he stepped into the dim light thrown by a nearby lamp. "Last I seen of him, he was doing some fixing at what used to was his place," one person offered.

"You mind pointing me in that direction?"

Another man pointed. "End of town there. It's the feed and grain place, or what's left of it."

Lon smiled, tipped his hat. "Thank you." He moved on, leading his horse.

Determined to prevail, Lon proceeded toward the ruins of the feed and grain warehouse. He identified it by the remnants of the sign in front of it and went into it, lifting the rifle to his shoulder. "Teverence, show yourself. I come to kill you."

He continued through the debris. The shuffling behind him caught Lon's attention. He turned, still holding the rifle at the ready. Two men stood about ten feet away, separated by six feet of space. Their sidearms were drawn and leveled on him.

"You put the rifle down, kid."

"You ain't killing nobody."

He was outnumbered and outgunned, but, although he was at a loss for what to do next, he stood his ground. Fear gripped him. He had stupidly put himself in a bind. Now he needed to cipher a way out of it.

The first man repeated his command. "I said put the gun down."

Lon's breath caught in his throat. His heart pounded heavily. He forced his mind to work. The men closed in from two sides. Panic set in as Lon's flight instinct took hold. With a sudden move, he turned and made a dive deeper into the wreckage where darkness provided some concealment. One of the men pegged a shot after him, scaring him even more. He landed hard on burned boards and rolled behind a still standing roof pillar, almost losing the rifle in the process. There he remained quiet, watching the men search for him. In the distance, voices called out seeking the whereabouts of the shot. He noted the voices becoming louder and coming closer. He had to get out of there.

As more people arrived, the two stalkers turned their attention momentarily away from Lon to update their companions, giving him his only chance. He scrambled away from the pillar, crawling deeper into the rubble. As his pursuers came straight at him, following the sounds he made, he circled them as quietly as he could, now heading for the street. Ten feet from his horse, he got up and scaled the waste, then ran to his horse. He pulled himself on and kicked the horse up to a gallop.

The townsmen turned back toward the street as Lon rode past them. One man raised his revolver and fired. A burning slash in his upper arm told Lon the ball had cut a swath and taken a chunk of flesh with it. Oh, God, he'd been shot.

He kicked the animal's flanks harder to push greater speed. Doing its best, the horse galloped though the street and into the countryside as more shots were fired. Uncertain whether he was being chased, Lon rode hard until the town was only a small image on the horizon, stopping only when the horse became too winded to go on.

In the middle of the Kansas wilderness, he stopped and slid off the horse, setting the rifle on the ground. Still shaking from the experience, he turned into the moonlight until he had enough illumination to examine the wound in his left arm. Blood streamed down his arm, staining the shirt sleeve. There was a piercing pain. Dried blood caused parts of the material above the gash to adhere to the wound. He lifted it for a better view, increasing the pain as the sleeve tore away new flesh. This had to be looked after, but he could do nothing here. He ripped away the lower sleeve and used it as a temporary bandage to slow the bleeding, tying the knot off with the aid of his teeth.

A sudden weakness in his knees required him to drop to a sitting position. He remained there until he settled down enough to get back on the horse. There was only one place he'd be welcome. Changing direction, he headed toward Toby Joe Hawks's cabin.

It was well after midnight when Lon arrived at Hawks's house. Exhausted, he made no attempt to be quiet as he rode up, not suspecting there would be consequences for that. His back was turned to the door as he got down. He dropped the horse's reins and held onto the rifle.

"Stay right where you are, stranger." Hawks's voice was even, threatening.

Lon froze. "Toby Joe, it's me, Lon."

"I know who you be. I knew it 'fore you even got close. If it weren't me standing here, you'd be dead right about now 'cause I'd a shot you with the gun I ain't holding. Shit, boy, you got to get your smarts going you expect to survive. You made enough noise out here to rouse the devil himself."

"Reckon I didn't think."

"Mighty well told. Well, don't just stand there. Put up your horse and come inside."

Lon took the reins and led the horse into the small stable enclosing Hawks's horse and tack. Hawks stepped back into the cabin. Lon, removing the horse's bridle, saw a light start in the house. After finishing with the horse, he left the stable and hurried into the cabin, holding his arm below the wound.

Hawks was seated at the small table in the center of the room. "What happened?"

"I got shot."

Hawks nodded. "Teverence fought back, eh?"

Lon went to the table and sat heavily across from Hawks. "No, sir, I never even got close to Teverence. Them folks in Shawneetown, they turned on me when I asked for him. Started shooting at me. I had to run for it."

"Could have told you as much. Matter of fact, I tried to tell you as much, but you wouldn't listen. Too full of hate for your own good."

Lon breathed a heavy sigh, continuing to favor his arm. "I'm sorry."

"Yes, you be. A sorry mess is what you be. Now, you can do one of two things. Get out right now and go get yourself killed, or you can listen to what I tell you and learn how to stay alive. Your choice."

Lon pondered for a second. "I'll listen to you, Toby Joe, I will."

"All right, then. Let's get that arm fixed up first. Stand up."

Lon obeyed. Hawks undid the bandage and brought the lamp close to the wound for a better examination. "Pretty deep. I'll clean it out first, but it's got to be 'caterized' so's it don't fester."

"Caterized?" Lon was puzzled. The word was unfamiliar to him.

"Singed by a hot iron till it closes up. Hurts like hell, leaves a hell of a mark, but leastwise you won't lose the arm."

"Oh, shit."

"Yup."

Hawks began to assemble the things he would need to work on the wound. "Seeing as how I ain't got nothing to dull the pain, get yourself ready for some hellacious hurting."

Lon sat down to endure the jabbing and swiping of Hawks's

heavy hand at washing out the gash. He tried to be a man about it and stifle the screams of pain aching to come out. But the poker was overwhelming. Hawks left it in the fire for the whole time it took to cleanse the dried blood as well as the bits of flesh the ball had left in its wake. Then, when it was red hot and glowing, Hawks laid it into the lesion and held it there while it seared its way to closing the injury. There was a second or two delay before Lon could not bear it any longer. At the top of his lungs, he let out a howl that might have woken the dead had there been any around. It lasted until his breath was expended. Then, after sucking in a great gulp of air, he did it again even louder, if such was possible. When Hawks, leaning heavily on Lon's hand to keep it in place, was satisfied the job was done, he pulled the poker away. The smoke and smell of burning flesh filled the cabin. Lon continued to holler, transitioning into cries, as the pain continued. Hawks dropped the poker into its receptacle near the fire as Lon's head fell back in complete collapse.

He felt Hawks unbuckle the gun belt from his hips and all but carry the boy to the cot in the corner of the room, the same bed Hawks used. Setting Lon onto it, he pulled him to his side, turning the wounded arm to face him. Lon passed out as Hawks began the bandaging process.

7

LON SLEPT UNTIL MID MORNING. He had been exhausted enough when he arrived at Hawks's place, but the ordeal of the wound being cleaned and cauterized put him over the edge. His sleep was almost catatonic. He stayed in the position in which Hawks had placed him until, many hours later, his eyes opened to a room filled with daylight.

Immediate pain shocked him awake, but there was no throbbing. As he became more aware, the pain was slightly less than it had been the night before. Slowly, he assessed his current situation. The arm was in a sling, no doubt provided by Toby Joe. The last he remembered fully was the god awful torment of that damn 'caterizing,' the odor of which still lingered in the cabin and in his nostrils. Everything else, the move to the bed, the bandaging, were fleeting glimpses before he fell into black. Now conscious, but still not completely alert, he tried, without moving much, to glance around.

Hawks sat at the table cutting a swath from a hide laid out across the table's surface and slung toward the floor. "Toby Joe," Lon's voice was weak, harsh.

Hawks looked up from his work. "Well now, 'spected you to be out longer'n this. You went down something fierce last night."

Lon groaned and tried to move, then changed his mind because of the difficulty and his lack of energy. He tried to speak but could not muster the strength his voice required either.

"You just lay there," Hawks said. "Get your bearings. You been through a heap. It'll take a spell to come back from that."

Lon forced a nod, a major effort in his condition, and closed his eyes. This sleep was more restful and lasted until midday. When he awoke, some of the pain had subsided, and he was ravenously hungry. As his senses returned and he began thinking again, the odor of cauterization had been displaced by the smell of bacon cooking. He glanced around to see Hawks tending a frying pan on the tiny stove. Numbly, he concluded the pan must have been where the bacon smell came from.

Clearing his throat, he raised himself on his good arm. "I surely got a hankering for some of that bacon." His speech was feeble.

"Coming right up."

In somewhat better spirits, Lon swung his body to a sitting position and attempted to stand up. Unsteady, he immediately fell back to the cot. Hawks hurried to him and put his arm under Lon's. With Hawks's help, Lon was able to stand and make his way to the table. They sat across from each other and ate the bacon, with Lon consuming the larger portion.

Hawks spoke as they ate. "Ain't safe you going back to your place. First place they'll check for you, and, make no mistake, they'll be searching for you, sure as hell. By now, Teverence knows you're after him, so he'll be looking to head you off. You be not only a personal threat to him, but, as a leader in Shawneetown and running the Jayhawkers, he can't leave you to stand against him. You be staying here a spell."

"But I ain't finished the planting yet." Lon still tried to hang on to his life as he knew it.

Hawks leaned closer. "And likely you ain't never going to. You got to see this is bigger'n that. What you done last night put you outside the law. And you done pissed Teverence off in the bargain. You done give him everything he needs to come after you legal-like. And when he gets ahold of you, he ain't letting go."

"So, I'll get him first."

"Aw, you still don't savvy, Lon." Hawks became agitated. "You won't even get near him, not now. He got everyone supporting him and protecting him, them thinking he's God's gift to Shawneetown. The only thing you can do is disappear for a spell. Stay here till you're healed a mite, then find someplace else to hang your hat. Your life depends on it." He leaned back in his chair. "Meantime, you can finish your training. That-a-way, when you do come back, you'll be ready for him, and he won't be expecting you. Or, like I said last night, you can just go on out now and get yourself killt."

Lon studied his friend and finally grasped the gravity of the situation. "You been right so far. I'll do like you say."

Hawks exhaled a breath of relief. "That's better. Now, you get your rest. We'll get back to training when you're up to it."

In the late afternoon, Hawks stepped out onto the porch for a breath of air after spending a few hours crafting an ornate belt. After a few seconds out there, he hurried back inside to fetch a spyglass.

Lon followed him back to the porch. "What you looking for?"

"That dust there. Riders." Pointing to the dot on the horizon, he showed Lon the direction from which they came.

"I'm ready." Lon put his hand on the butt of his holstered revolver.

"No, you ain't. You do anything against Teverence now, with his friends around, and no matter what you say, they'll shoot you down or hang you. You got to stay clear of him till you can get him alone, when he ain't expecting it. Just you and him, no witnesses.

Now, you get yourself behind the stable, and you stay there. I'll get rid of 'em."

"But—"

"Lon, you said you'd listen to me, so you listen now. Do like I say, and you'll live to square it with Teverence later."

"All right."

Hawks used the glass to finally identify some of the participants. "Teverence, Daylock. Yeah, and there's Old Sam. And they loaded for bear. Get yourself hid. Now!"

Without a word, Lon made for the stable, moving behind it to completely to obscure him from view. There he waited, pistol in hand.

Hawks turned and hurried into the cabin. Lon watched as he reached the Henry rifle from its mooring above the doorway. Placing it against the inner wall, he stood in the door within easy reach of the weapon.

A tense few minutes passed while the group approached. Hawks tried to strike a nonchalant pose to allay suspicions, all the while ready to reach out the Henry and put it in play.

The riders entered the yard and pulled up at Teverence's direction. Hawks leaned against the door frame, favoring his bum leg.

"How do, Teverence. What brings you all the way out here?"

Teverence completed his visual examination of the area before answering. "Looking for the Pearce kid. I hear he threatened to kill me, even come into town fixing to do it. I ain't sitting still for that. You seen him?"

Hawks feigned a surprised expression. "Can't say I have. Ain't seen none of the Pearces in quite a spell." He slapped at his stiffened limb. "Leg don't let me get around too good of late. Been bothering me more with the coming-on of cooler weather. You know how it be."

"I reckon." Teverence seemed unsatisfied. He scrutinized the area again, shifting in his saddle. "You sure you ain't seen him?"

Still behind the stable, Lon placed his thumb on the hammer of the revolver in preparation to engage it if necessary. His breath quickened as he expected the worst.

Hawks nodded. "What I done said."

"Well, all right, but you keep an eye peeled. The kid's got him some guns, so I'd peg him dangerous."

"I'll watch out. I surely will."

Teverence sat there for a second studying Hawks. "Well, all right. You take care now, hear?"

Hawks cracked a broad, engaging smile. "You do the same."

Teverence made a grunt of disappointment and pulled his horse around. The group followed suit, and they started out, heading in the direction from which they came. Hawks remained in position until they were well out of sight. When he was satisfied, he stepped into the yard. "Lon."

Lon responded to the call, stepping from his position while holstering his weapon. Hawks limped to meet him halfway.

"You reckon they swallowed that?"

"Maybe, maybe not. But we ain't wasting no more time. You start training right now for good and all."

From there on, Lon followed Hawks's instructions. Hawks took him through learning to shoot faster with both pistol and rifle, then, as his health and agility improved, he taught him to fire accurately from a moving horse.

Lon quickly became adept at working through random scenarios posed to him by Hawks. He learned point and shoot techniques which greatly increased his speed and accuracy, finally arriving at the ability to think through and extricate himself from any situation Hawks could concoct.

In the yard after completing his final exercise a week and a half later, Lon reloaded the revolver. Hawks thought for a moment. "I don't reckon they's much more I can learn you. You can fend for yourself now. It's time you got out of Kansas, leastwise till things cool down."

"I ain't never been nowheres else but here, Toby Joe. I don't know where to go."

"I been pondering on that myself. You can head south to Texas. They got them big cattle ranches down there. You can get work there, learn a trade. I hear cowboying's pretty steady work. Pay ain't great, but it'll get you by."

"What about the farm?"

"Reckon you can forget the farm. Teverence'll be constant watching there. You show up there, you're a dead man. You can take that to the bank."

Lon became distraught. "But the farm's everything we got." Even now he had not accepted the loss of his parents, the complete loss of his previous life. His hand went to the back of his head in disbelief.

Hawks placed a hand on Lon's shoulder. "Lon, I hate to remind you, but you got to face the fact, they ain't no more *we*. They's only you, and you ain't no more got nothing but the clothes on your back. You got to make a life for yourself best way you can, boy, in some other place. And you got to go fast. Now."

Lon turned away, not wanting to face the inevitable. He paced the yard for several seconds, his hand still behind his neck. Slowly, he accepted the fact. He had no choice. He turned to face Hawks. "Reckon I'm going."

"Good man. Let's get you ready for the trail."

Lon followed Hawks into the stable.

"Saddle up."

"Toby Joe, now you know I don't own no saddle."

"Yeah, you do. Take mine. I got another one almost done."

By now, knowing better than to argue with his friend, Lon grabbed the saddle and laid it on his horse's back. Hawks picked up saddlebags hanging on a stall wall and headed for the cabin as Lon led his horse out of the stable.

From inside the house, a minute later, Hawks emerged with the saddlebags burgeoning with ammunition and canned goods. He carried the Sharps carbine under his arm and limped as he secured the bag straps. When he reached Lon, he handed him the long gun. Lon inserted it into the saddle scabbard. Then Hawks gave the boy the saddlebags. "They's enough in there to get you about a week across Kansas. Reckon the rest be up to you."

Hawks dug into his trousers pocket and brought out a gold coin. "Take this case you run short of things."

Lon looked at the coin. A double eagle. "This is too much, Toby Joe. What's in here's enough to get me by."

"Little insurance." Hawks placed the coin in Lon's hand.

Reluctantly, Lon pocketed the money. He placed and secured the bags behind the saddle.

Loss became apparent again, similar to the sinking feeling he had experienced at the deaths of his parents. He was leaving the only place he had ever known as home. And he was leaving the closest person he now had to a parent. It overwhelmed him. He turned to Hawks with an expression betraying his inner feelings but found it next to impossible to speak. After a few seconds of standing there, he cleared his throat and forced out what he needed to say. "Toby Joe, I... I ain't never going to be able to thank you enough for what you done. Nor repay you."

"No need to."

Almost in tears, Lon grabbed his friend in an awkward hug.

"Good chance we won't see each other again, boy." Hawks held him a step back. "So you take care of yourself. Remember what I learned you. And don't never point them guns at no one you ain't willing to shoot. If you do, make it count. You don't get no second chances. And don't let 'em rile you. Keep your head... and you'll keep your head."

"I'll remember. And I'll never forget you and all you done."

"You'd best get moving. No telling when Teverence might be back. Still plenty of daylight left to get you a fur piece from here. Keep going and go live your life."

"Yes, sir." Lon wiped a hand across his eyes, but he did not move. He seemed anchored in place.

"Go on." Hawks waved the back of his hand at Lon. "Get on out of here 'fore you get me to blubbering, too."

That motivated Lon. He mounted up and pulled the horse around, setting out on his journey, heading southwest in search of a new life.

8

MORE GUNFIRE SENT SLUGS INTO and near the tree as Lackamore pulled the gun from his waistband while Shawnee returned shots. Ostro and two men from inside the tent crouched behind a table they had hauled outside to use as cover. They fired wildly and profusely, apparently unskilled in the use of firearms. It seemed they were just hoping their shots would hit their marks. Shawnee, on the other hand, recalling Toby Joe Hawks's training, conserved ammunition and tried to make every shot count.

From the opposite side of the tree, Lackamore joined the fight and attempted to mimic his young companion's actions. Quickly, this brought their attackers to the point of reloading, almost at the same time, creating a dry spot in their assault.

Shawnee took advantage of it. "They're reloading. Get your horse and get out of here. I'll keep them down."

"No, I can't leave you here."

Shawnee became adamant. "You got a daughter. I got no one. Do like I say!"

Lackamore got up and made a dash for his horse, which had stopped a few yards away. Shawnee peaked out from the side of the tree, glanced at the upturned table, and then scanned for nearby cover. He settled on an outcropping of boulders to his right and set out for them as Lackamore mounted and galloped off in the opposite direction.

Ostro and his cohorts rose almost as one, ready to fire. Lackamore disappeared in the distance, out of pistol range. Shawnee ran for the rocks.

Ostro pointed with the barrel of his gun. "Get that one."

His posse scrambled around the table and went to a dead run after Shawnee.

Reaching the boulders with an empty revolver, Shawnee climbed quickly and searched for a secluded spot in which to reload. He dropped between two large rocks and went through the lengthy reloading procedure required by percussion pistols as he watched his assailants reach the rocks and start their ascent.

Having loaded six rounds instead of the customary five, Shawnee leaned out and drew a bead on the man closest to him. This man looked up from his climb and spotted Shawnee. Shawnee's shot caught him in the shoulder and spun him off the boulder to fall several feet down. Immediately, Shawnee went farther up the boulder until he found a narrow opening between the rocks, a natural hiding spot. Ostro fired a shot at him, but it missed. He watched from his position as Ostro and the other man kept coming, noticing that Ostro lagged behind, seemingly out of breath.

Concentrating on the man in front, Shawnee took careful aim and fired a ball into the man's upper leg, dropping him to the ground and eliciting screams of pain. Shawnee turned away and kept climbing until he reached the top of the highest boulder. Then he began a hasty descent down the far side, losing sight of Ostro.

His strength waning, Shawnee slid down the final section of rock, bringing him to level ground. He took a second to catch his breath, then started a trot around the perimeter of the boulders and back toward the torn away picket line. Searching as he moved, he located his horse, standing and grazing near the big gray with the fancy saddle. He ran in a straight line toward his mount. People from inside the tent milled around the overturned table. They did not appear to pose a threat. Shawnee reckoned most folks don't want to get involved in a shooting. He continued to the horse and slowed as he reached it to prevent spooking the animal.

As he reached for the reins, a shot whizzed past his head, causing the horse to shy back. He turned and raised the Colt. Ostro ran, with great effort, toward him. Reflex action cocked and fired Shawnee's gun. The ball drilled squarely into Ostro's chest, pushing him back several inches and sprawling him out on his back. He moved erratically for a second, then he was still.

Shawnee stared at the scene before him. Shit! I killed him. Transfixed, he stood motionless, still in the firing position he had assumed when he pulled the trigger. Then the realization took hold. He had just taken a life. Maybe it was justified, and maybe Ostro deserved it, but he had taken a life all the same. He killed a fellow man. Oddly, Toby Joe's warning, "Don't never point them guns at no one you ain't willing to shoot. If you do, make it count," came to mind. He had aimed his two previous hits, wanting only to wound, to stop their advance, but this—this was something else. Uncertain if this was intentional or just a lucky, or, for Ostro, an unlucky shot, Shawnee realized he had crossed the line. Whether it was fair or not, he'd taken a life, and he would have to live with that from here on.

As his stomach began to churn over this, he glanced to his left at the crowd in front of the tent. There was fear in them, fear of the possibility of him turning his gun on them. They shrank back, some retreating inside the tent. Taking several deep breaths to keep his insides down, he holstered the pistol and turned toward his horse. His legs were a little wobbly as he walked carefully toward the animal. He hauled in one final cleansing breath and reached again for the reins. "Whoa, boy, whoa." He climbed into the saddle. As the horse turned, the gray came into Shawnee's view. Surely is a fine animal. Ostro ain't going to no more need him. Shawnee directed his mount to the gray horse and picked up its reins. "Easy, there," he said quietly. He untied the reins from the rope and looked back at the people near the tent. Some now hurried to examine Ostro while the others ducked back inside the tent. They had just seen him kill a man and take his horse. There was no turning back now. Leading the gray behind him, he set out at a fast pace in the direction Lackamore had taken.

As soon as he was out of sight of the tent, Shawnee pulled up and examined his new possession. He found in the saddle scabbard a Henry repeating rifle, the same gun Toby Joe spoke so highly about. Rummaging through the saddlebags, he turned up several boxes of cartridges for the Henry. He transferred the contents of his own saddlebags to the new ones. Already having observed the gray's responsiveness during the ride, he now checked over the horse itself, observing muscle structure and teeth. Satisfied this was a strong, healthy animal, he remounted his own horse and moved on, leading the gray along with them.

Following his instincts and watching for landmarks he had observed in his trip from the farm, Shawnee arrived there in the late afternoon. As he rode toward the farmhouse, he saw Lackamore exiting the house with two rifles under his arm. Marcy followed as Lackamore walked to his waiting horse. Then Marcy turned and saw Shawnee riding in. She pointed to Shawnee and said something to her father. Lackamore focused on where she indicated. Shawnee reined in close to them and dismounted.

"I was going to head back to help you."

"No need. It's handled."

"Are you all right? How did you—"

Shawnee scrambled to word the answer so Marcy would not learn the details. "The how ain't important. Just know Ostro won't bother you no more."

Lackamore seemed to grasp the meaning of Shawnee's statement. He nodded. "I guess I should never have gone there in the first place. I had no idea what I was getting into."

"Lesson learned, I reckon."

"Well, I can't thank you enough for jumping in. I don't even know what to call you."

"He's called Shawnee." Marcy spoke up with a smile.

"Sounds kind of odd. Don't you—"

"Shawnee's all you need to know. Won't be staying long enough to get acquainted."

"But we owe you so much. *I* owe you so much. At least let us feed you."

"Please, Shawnee."

"Wished I could, but they's some folks back there ain't going to take too kindly to what I done. And some folks on back a them, as well, truth be told. Don't want to bring none of that down on you. Best I move on right quick."

Shawnee squatted in front of Marcy. "Now, Marcy, you be sure the next body you drop a hay bale on is friendly-like, you hear?" A grin accompanied his words.

Marcy chuckled. "I will."

Shawnee pushed his hat back and handed his horse's reins to Marcy. "Now, this here fellow behind me, he's kind of old, and he ain't too fast, but he's gentle enough, so you take good care of him, will you?"

Marcy was surprised. "Wait, you're giving me your horse?"

Shawnee nodded. "Seeing as how he needs a good home and I need a fast horse and Mister Ostro ain't going to be needing his no more, you take this one, and I'll take the gray."

Marcy took the reins. "I... I don't know what to say."

"I reckon a thank you will do 'er."

"Shawnee, are you sure you want to do this?"

Shawnee looked up at Lackamore. "Yes, sir, I am."

"And the saddle and rifle?"

"The gray's got everything I need. You're welcome to the rest."

Marcy wrapped her arms around Shawnee's neck, almost toppling him, and planted a kiss on his cheek. "Thank you, Shawnee."

"You are very welcome." Shawnee said as Marcy stepped back. He rose and faced Lackamore. "Reckon you be shed a gambling by now. If you need extra money to get by, you might want to consider selling the horse and rig."

"Oh, I'm done with gambling, all right, thanks to you. But we'll get by on what we've got. I won't sell Marcy's gift, not for anything."

"Glad to hear it." Shawnee went to the gray and mounted. "You two, you're all you got. You take good care of each other." He yanked down on his hat, pulled the horse around, and rode out.

Marcy waved and called after him. "Goodbye, Shawnee."

9

STILL A SHAMBLES AFTER SEVERAL weeks of rebuilding, Shawneetown was a beehive of activity. The sounds of construction filled the air as its citizens, those who were left, tried to resume their lives.

Carl Teverence oversaw the clearing of the collapsed structure which had housed his feed and grain business, but, in the back of his mind, the untimely death of Isabel Pearce and the disappearance of the Pearce kid would not let up. At crossed purposes, he hoped against hope he would never be placed at the scene of her death, but his desire to administer justice to Lon for the kid's attempt on his life was all consuming. He was too important to the life of this town to allow it to stand.

As he observed the progress of the work on his lot, Otto Daylock stepped up beside him. Daylock indicated the operation in front of them. "Carl. How's it going?"

Teverence huffed. "Too slow. Frame shoulda been up by now." He glanced at Old Sam, hunched at Daylock's side. "You just get back?"

"Yep." Sam seemed tuckered. "Didn't find nothing. Covered a good fifty mile in ever direction. He ain't been seed nowheres."

Teverence let out a long breath. "Every day goes by, that boy gets harder to find."

"Why we still trying to find him, anyways?" Daylock asked. "He never come close to laying a hand on you. Why not let it go?"

"'Cause it ain't right, that's why. It ain't right he made the try at me, just like it ain't right what his pa done. And the kid knowed about where his pa'd went. That was proved when we found that plow hid, and it being all in one piece and not broke and all. What ain't right's got to be rectified, Otto, and the offenders taken to task so nobody else tries it. We're nothing if we ain't got right on our side and we don't stand up for it. Sooner or later, the kid'll pay for his transgressions. I won't rest till he does."

OVER THE NEXT SEVERAL WEEKS, Shawnee and his new companion, which he now called Gray, became closer. He made sure not to overtax the horse, riding at easy paces unless a harder ride became absolutely necessary, and he made Gray's care a priority, brushing and currying the animal whenever possible. Before Shawnee ate, the animal ate. Before Shawnee drank, he made sure Gray was watered. As time passed, a bond formed between the two. The horse stayed in close proximity to him during idle times. With no human company available, Shawnee took to talking to the horse. His quiet conversations generated nickers and nuzzles from Gray and provided Shawnee with a much needed closeness as well as a pastime. He spoke of nothing in particular, but his tone was always pleasant and engaging. Shawnee wondered if Ostro had mistreated Gray. Nothing was evident, but Shawnee's short acquaintance with Ostro told him the man had been capable of that and much more. "Well, if he did, it's all over and done with now."

On a well-worn road in southwest Kansas, Shawnee rode at a little

more than a walk, keeping an eye peeled for the nearest town or settlement. A previous stop several days earlier had garnered only a few
canned goods, necessitating another replenishment to keep him going.
He proceeded on this trail instead of staying on less travelled roads in
the hope it would lead to a larger, more well stocked community.

As he scanned the horizon in front of him, a rumbling sound
coming from behind him seized his attention. He pulled Gray up and
glanced back. In the distance, but coming on quickly, a buckboard
drawn by two galloping horses came into view. Squinting for a better
view, he made out the form of a woman on the seat. Her actions and
the fact there seemed to be no reins in her hands indicated the team
was out of control. It showed no signs of slowing as it approached.

The wagon thundered toward him. The woman hung on to
the seat to prevent being pitched off as the vehicle careened and
bounced from the imperfections in the road. As it passed, the woman screamed out for help several times. The reins were nowhere to
be seen. Likely they'd fallen into the frenzy of the team. This was a
runaway for sure. He urged Gray forward and set out at a gallop to
catch up and try to stop it.

Loosening his hold on the reins, Shawnee gave the horse its head,
"Go, Gray, go!" and Gray's speed impressed him. Even at the greater pace, it took close to a quarter mile before he came alongside the
team. Reaching neck and neck with the lead team horse, Shawnee
reached out and grabbed its bridle strap. Immediately, he hauled back
on Gray's reins and held his grip on the bridle, pulling the team out of
their gallop and eventually to a breathless halt.

Dropping from the saddle, he scrambled to retrieve the team's
reins which were tangled into the rigging. He spoke quieting words to
the horses as he pulled the reins free and glanced back at the seat to see
the woman frozen in place. She had a pleasant face which seemed able

to radiate a beaming smile, although at present it bore an expression of flat-out fear. He guessed her age to be at around his mother's, just needing to be a little taller and less plump. She wore a gingham dress and matching sunbonnet.

Shawnee collected the reins, untangled them, and pulled them over the heads of the horses. He moved to the woman. "Ma'am, you all right?"

Her hands were still locked onto the seat. Her body shook visibly, and she struggled to catch her breath. Finally, she spoke. "I… I think so. Thank you."

"Yes, ma'am. You was moving powerful fast there." Shawnee smiled and handed up the reins, but she did not move to take them. "It's all right. They should be calmed down now and plumb wore out, as well."

The woman let go of the seat and reached the reins from Shawnee's hand. "I was trying to get to town to get help. Something spooked the horses, a rattler I think, but I lost the reins. I couldn't control them. I have to hurry."

Shawnee perceived the shakiness and frenetic quality in her voice, which raised his concern more was wrong than just the runaway. "What kind of help you going after?"

"A boy fell into a well back a ways. We can't get him out."

"How far's the town?"

"About five miles."

"How far back's the well?"

"About a mile or so."

"Well, ma'am, you go ahead on to the town. I'll go back there and see if I can help."

The woman's demeanor changed dramatically. Her expression became less intense. "Oh, thank you. It's off the road to the right. You can't miss it."

Shawnee said no more. He hurried to Gray and stepped on as the horse began moving. He called Gray to an immediate gallop as the woman gently and tentatively snapped the reins on the backs of her team, taking her in the opposite direction. As she moved away, she drove the horses to higher speed.

The gray moved quickly down the trail as Shawnee scanned the area to the right. In the distance, the chaotic scene at the well came into his view. He guided the horse off the trail to cover the short stretch ahead as fast as possible. During this sprint, several women and children milled around what he took to be the well. Their presence around it made it difficult for him to see the object clearly, but he allowed his assumption to prevail. They seemed highly concerned, moving about and craning over something. Shawnee, through fleeting glimpses, made out the stone walls of the well and the feeble wood construction of the support bar for the dipping instrument. They were peering into the well. At one point, he saw there was no rope attached to the crossbar. He rode in and stopped abruptly, drawing the bystanders' attention. He dismounted and moved quickly to their midst. "I run into the lady driving the wagon on the trail back there. I come to help."

In reply, many voices spoke at once, making it impossible for him to understand any of them. "Hold on now, folks. You got to talk one at a time. Now the lady back there says there's a little boy fell into the well."

"He's my son...Jason." The woman who spoke stepped from within the crowd. She was slight, and her face appeared weather beaten with dark eyes and thin lips. "He's only four." Distress was evident on her face and in her speech.

She seemed a tad old to be the mother of a four-year-old, but life out here on the prairie was pretty rough. It could age a body quick. She was distraught, and Shawnee sought to calm her. "Let's see if we can get him out a there. Can you talk to him?"

"Yes, but he's so scared he's not making sense."

Shawnee moved to the well wall, which came to his waist. He peered over. "Jason," he said loudly. "Can you hear me?"

"Get me out," the boy's voice called through crying. "It's dark. I can't see nothing."

"I'll get you out, Jason." Shawnee's reply was more to calm the boy than to say he knew how he would accomplish this. "Just stay calm. Don't be afraid. I'll get you out." Shawnee quickly observed the wood structure. He turned to the crowd. "Where's the bucket rope?"

"It's in the well." This came from one of the children, a boy who appeared to be about the same age as Jason. "We was horsing around, and Jason climbed up on the well and jumped into the bucket. The rope let go, and he fell in, and the rope went in after him."

"We don't have another rope." a female voice added.

Shawnee's mind began to work. He needed means to get to the boy if he was going to bring him out. A quick glance told him the crossbar would not be stout enough to support the weight of a man. There was a rope on his newly acquired saddle. He searched the area for something to use in place of the crossbar. A tree a few yards away offered a solution. He trotted back to Gray and climbed on. As he directed the horse toward the tree, the eyes of the onlookers followed him. He loosed the lariat from its strapping and selected a branch on the tree he estimated to be strong enough. He also estimated the length of the now uncurled rope at about thirty feet. He hoped that'd be enough.

Looping the rope over the branch, he wrapped the other end around his saddle horn and stroked Gray's flanks with his heels. The horse started forward but stopped when the branch offered resistance. "Come on, Gray. Pull on it, boy, pull it down." At Shawnee's urging, Gray moved forward and kept tension on the rope. Shawnee pulled up on the reins, causing Gray to rear up. Pushing with its hide legs, Gray lunged forward. The branch snapped and fell to the ground.

Returning to the well, dragging the branch behind, Shawnee dismounted and hauled the branch as close to the well as he could. He moved the rope to the center and tied it off securely, at the same time dropping his hat on the ground. "Some of you folks give me a hand to get this across the wall?"

The hands of the ten females joined Shawnee's effort to lift the branch and place it across the well. He gave the thing a shove to make certain it was seated. Then he sent the rest of the rope into the well. Scooting up to sit on the wall, he turned himself so his feet were dangling over the opening. Reaching for the rope, he wrapped it around his hand a few turns, yanked tight on it. Then he dropped himself into the hole coming to an abrupt halt a few feet down when the rope pulled taut.

His weight caused the rope to pinch his hand. Light at this level became noticeably less. He would need to conduct the rest of this in relative darkness. As he gripped the rope with his legs and repositioned his hands to be able to climb, he closed his eyes to try to acclimate them to the low level of light.

"Jason." He listened for the answer.

The boy hollered back. "Yeah?"

"Hang on, I'm coming for you."

Climbing down hand over hand with the support of his legs, Shawnee moved slowly, closing his eyes frequently. "Jason, keep hollering at me."

"What's your name, mister?"

"Shawnee."

"What did you say? Sore knee?"

Shawnee raised his voice and spoke slower to be better understood across the distance. "That'll do, Jason, that'll do." His plan was to keep the boy talking to take his mind off his situation and to pinpoint his location. As he descended into the darkness, the boy's thrashing around in the water became audible.

Jason continued to call out. "It's cold!"

"I'm still coming, Jason. Hang on."

"It's scary down here!"

"Won't be long now. I'm almost there."

The end of the rope slipped through Shawnee's legs. He couldn't run out of rope now. A few more inches and his boots touched the water. "Jason, reach around. See if you can find my boots. They're in the water."

Splashing sounds increased as the boy followed the instructions. In a few seconds, Shawnee felt small hands gripping at his boots.

"I got 'em." Jason's voice was breathless.

Shawnee wrapped the rope around his hand. "Hang on with one hand and reach up with your other hand. Reach as high as you can. I'm going to try to grab your hand."

Jason did as he was told. Shawnee lowered his free hand and moved it about in an attempt to locate and grasp the boy's arm. The elapsing time seemed endless as the rope dug into Shawnee's hand and cut off circulation to his fingers. Then his hand brushed past Jason's, barely touching. He immediately reversed direction and found the tiny hand with a slap.

A quick clutch on Jason's arm secured the catch. Shawnee used whatever strength he had left to lift the boy straight up. Water drained from Jason's body and clothing as Shawnee pulled Jason up and out and lifted him to the level of his own chest. Shawnee grunted as he pulled the boy into position. "I got you, Jason, I got you. Now reach out in front of you. Feel for my chest and shoulders." As he spoke, he placed Jason's arm around his own neck. Jason followed instructions. "Now find your other hand and lock them together back there."

A few seconds passed as Jason felt around in the darkness, located his hands, and linked his fingers around Shawnee's neck. "All right, now," Shawnee whispered as he wrapped his arm around Jason's back and pulled the boy to him. "Don't you let go."

"I... I won't."

Turning his head skyward, Shawnee shouted. "Hey, up there. I got him. Grab hold of the rope. Pull us up."

A second went by like an hour. Shawnee felt tugs on the rope, uncertain at first, then more secure yanks. He was pulled against the wall of the well as people above positioned the rope so they could brace themselves and bring him up. It was slow. He kept his back to the wall to prevent injury to Jason. This caused painful bumping and dragging to his own body. His rope ensnared hand lost feeling. Then the arm became limp and was pulled straight up. He hoped the wrap around his hand held through the trip up.

A jagged stone in the wall caught the seam in the back of his shirt and ripped the fabric. For a fleeting second, it startled him, but once he determined it did not take flesh with it, he discounted it. He concentrated on his hold on Jason. "Hang on, Jason, we're getting there." The boy was blubbering. Shawnee's words elicited a giggle from him. Shawnee chalked that up to relief the ordeal was coming to an end.

They were pulled up far enough to come into low light. Shawnee saw the boy but found he was too close to actually make out Jason's features. It would wait. Time for looking later.

With his back to the people on the ground, Shawnee could not see their faces, but their grunts were evident as they put out a great effort to haul their cargo home. Shawnee said a silent thank you for the fact the rope was holding up, the same rope that now crippled his hand. Then multiple hands reached, gripped both his clothes and his arm as his neck became level with the top of the wall. He shouted at them. "Get Jason. Take the boy."

Other hands reached to take Jason and pull him from Shawnee, up and over the wall to safety. Then hands grabbed Shawnee's good arm. Hands full of his clothes secured him from falling and pulled him up onto the wall to a sitting position.

He sat there, catching lost breath, feeling the wetness transferred from Jason's body to his own, experiencing the tingling sensation in his hand as the women removed the rope.

Rubbing the feeling back into the hand took several moments. His shoulder joint and arm throbbed with pain. Moving the limb satisfied him nothing serious had been done to it. It'd heal over time.

He turned to see Jason's mother hugging and fawning over her son. The boy was now wrapped in a blanket. His mother, sitting on the ground, rocked him as he cried somewhat uncontrollably. Shawnee let out a sigh of relief as he swung his feet over the wall and slid off onto unsteady legs. He took a second to steady himself, then moved slowly to where the tearful mother cradled her son.

"H… how's he doing?"

The mother looked up at him. "I think he's all right. I don't think he's hurt, just shook up some." Her voice was shaky.

Shawnee smiled. "Boys're tough, ma'am. He'll make it through."

She stumbled over her next attempt to speak. "I can't… I… you.…" She shook her head. "I don't even know your name."

"It's Shawnee, ma'am, just Shawnee."

She composed herself. "Mister Shawnee, I'm Mary Winslow, and this is my son, Jason. I… we can't thank you enough for what you did."

Shawnee was suddenly at a loss for words. "Yes, ma'am," was all he could muster.

The other women crowded around, praising Shawnee's courage

and determination. He smiled and continued to rub feeling back into his hand and work his arm. One of the women brought him his hat. He thanked her as he shoved it on his head.

In that time, Mrs. Winslow got up and picked Jason up in her arms. The boy had stopped crying, and he had a smile on his face now. She walked to Shawnee, allowing Shawnee to finally see the face of the boy he just saved. "How're you doing, Jason?"

Jason smiled back. "I'm fine, Mister Shawnee. Thank you for saving me."

He'd likely been prompted by his mother, but, Shawnee reckoned, she just put words to what the boy was feeling.

"You ain't going to be playing around wells no more, are you?"

"No, sir."

"You're a good boy, Jason. You done exactly like I told you down there. I'm right glad to make your acquaintance, both of you."

"We came out here to have a picnic." Mrs. Winslow looked around at the crowd. "Won't you join us? It seems the least we can do to thank you."

Just as Shawnee was about to reply, attention was drawn to a group approaching on horseback. On closer observation as they drew nearer, Shawnee made out about a half dozen men. Behind these, the same buckboard Shawnee had stopped on the road was driven by the same woman. She likely made it to the town and roused help. Shawnee reserved the answer to Mrs. Winslow's question until the group arrived.

Some confusion ensued as the men dismounted and crowded in, asking questions too quickly to be answered properly. Then, one man, a heavy set individual in his mid-forties who wore a badge on his shirt, took charge. "All right, quiet down, folks," the man said in a growl. "Let's find out what's going on here."

Mrs. Winslow, still cradling Jason, stepped forward. "Everything's fine now, Nat. Jason and Saul were playing a little rough, and Jason fell into the well. Mister Shawnee risked his life to get Jason out." As she spoke, she indicated Shawnee.

Nat looked at Shawnee carefully, then stepped closer. "Well, peers like we owe you a vote of thanks, young fellow. Shawnee is it? What's the rest of it? Your name I mean."

"Shawnee's all, all that's needed."

Nat stroked his chin. "Hmmm."

Mrs. Winslow interrupted. "I just asked Mister Shawnee to stay for our picnic. He didn't have a chance to answer."

Nat changed his tone. "Sorry. Just natural curious is all. Go ahead, Shawnee, answer up."

Shawnee felt threatened by Nat. He had considered staying and enjoying some company and, perhaps, some good food at this picnic. That was before the men arrived. He was put off by Nat's "natural curious." If he allowed himself to be subjected to Nat's suspicious nature, more might come out than he'd want to be known. "I surely thank you for the invite, but I reckon I'll be moving on. There's places I got to be."

"But how will we ever be able to thank you?" Mrs. Winslow seemed beside herself.

"No thanks necessary, ma'am. I just done what anyone else'd do. I had a rope and a horse, and you folks didn't. Wasn't nothing."

"You saved my son's life. You can't call what you did nothing."

"Ma'am, I just got lucky is all. Best I be on my way." Shawnee pulled his hat down and moved to Gray, waiting nearby.

"God bless you, Shawnee," Mrs. Winslow said as he mounted.

"Thank you, ma'am." Shawnee pulled Gray around to face the trail. "That surely will help." He headed back to the trail and set out southwest, deciding he would avoid the town ahead as well. Besides the sore arm and torn shirt, he left with knowing his actions saved a young life and brought a family back together. All summed, not a bad day's work!

10

WITH THE POSSIBILITY OF TEVERENCE trailing him still fresh in his mind, Shawnee limited stops to restocking, never staying in one place long enough to allow the possibility of being found out. In truth, he had not seen any sign of Teverence since the day he left Hawks's place, yet he had no idea how much power the man wielded outside the confines of Shawneetown. It was conceivable Teverence had contacts throughout Kansas who might be on the lookout for him. Whether true or not, Shawnee could not risk taking the chance. He had to keep moving.

Signs along major roads he wandered onto during his journey indicated he was getting close to the border between Kansas and the Indian Territory. Shawnee knew very little about that region save for the fact sections of it were said to be a haven for law breakers and hunted men and boasted no organized law enforcement. It was established as a dumping spot for displaced Indians but soon attracted all manner of no-goods as well. While still aiming for Texas, Shawnee felt fairly comfortable he would likely be relatively safe traversing the Indian Territory, safer, at least, than he would be anywhere in Kansas.

His crossing into the Territory was uneventful as was his first several days of travel. Carrying a full complement of supplies and ammunition acquired at his last stop in Kansas, he avoided settlements and kept to back trails. About a week into the area, the terrain changed. The presence of more rock formations and hill country presented better hiding and cover if those became necessary to elude unwanted visitors. His camps were always established on higher ground, now that it was available, to provide sharper observation.

The camp in a flat spot on a hill gave Shawnee a view of the full area below. Early morning found him breaking camp and packing up to move on. Suddenly, rapid gunfire in the distance grabbed his attention. Staying alert and informed was paramount to his survival. This fact drew him to scan the ground below to determine the origin and reason for the shots. To observe unseen, he knelt behind a large boulder.

A lone horseman rode into the area at full gallop, followed at a dangerously close distance by four riders. Frequent but inaccurate shots were exchanged between them. The man being chased was at a distinct disadvantage, having to fire behind him.

Shawnee's first instinct was to remain the observer, but his sense of fair play caused him to recognize the lead rider's plight. The likelihood of the rider fleeing from the law seemed remote in this region. Four against one weren't right. Shawnee went to his already saddled horse and climbed on. He directed Gray toward the trail and set out at a gallop for the disturbance.

His mind worked quickly as he approached the rider, realizing the man might mistake him for an additional attacker. Before becoming visible to the man, he sought out an outcropping of rocks and pulled in off the road to dismount. Pulling the Henry from its saddle scabbard, he dropped into a kneeling position behind the rocks, shouldered the rifle, and levered the initial round into the chamber.

As the pursued man rode past and the four chasers came into range, Shawnee aimed at the one out front and fired. The recoil came straight back into his shoulder, and the man slumped in the saddle as the round pierced his upper body. Shawnee immediately followed the shot with four more, haphazardly aimed, which missed but scared and disbursed the remaining horsemen. They pulled up sharply and then scurried off in several different directions, leaving their wounded cohort clinging to his horse's neck as the horse strayed off the trail.

Shawnee stood up and moved out from cover, ready to continue firing, but the three who had fled were now out of range and showed no sign of returning. The wounded man slipped from his saddle to the ground. Quiet resumed, enough so the hoof beats behind him were easily made out. He turned, still ready to fire.

Closing quickly, the pursued rider kept a steady gallop, his pistol poised at shoulder height, pointed up at the ready. Within a few feet of Shawnee, he pulled hard rein and stopped, raising dust. Shawnee stood his ground.

The man was tall. That was evident even on the horse. Slim and lanky, he was well into his fifties. His face was whiskered and lined with age and weathering. He wore a buckskin jacket and striped range pants. The wide-brimmed dark hat was pulled down tight on his head but still allowed bushy, gray-white hair to spill out the sides. He relaxed in the saddle and lowered his weapon. "Don't know why you took a hand there, but I surely thank you." His speech was slow and measured, his voice deep and resonant.

Shawnee lowered his rifle. "Peered like you was outnumbered and outgunned. Didn't seem right to stand by. What were they after?"

"I didn't stop to ask. They came on me with their guns out, so I hightailed it."

"Good choice, I reckon."

The man holstered his revolver and dismounted, wearily. "My name's Bruno Tell." He extended his hand.

"Shawnee." Shawnee shook his hand.

"Again, thanks. I don't think I'd have survived without your help. My horse was giving out."

Shawnee smiled. "Glad to help. You reckon they'll come back?"

"I wouldn't if I was them." Tell indicated the man Shawnee shot. "Wonder if that one's still alive."

"Looked like I hit him dead center. I ain't concerned enough to find out, are you?"

"Nope." Tell regarded him with a long gaze. "Where're you headed?"

"Texas."

Tell nodded. "So am I. Where in Texas?"

"Nowheres in particular. Wherever I can find work."

Tell took a moment to give Shawnee a once-over. "Got a proposition for you. I own a spread outside Fort Worth. We're always looking for help. Ride along with me, and we'll see what we can put together for you."

"I been going it alone quite a spell. I don't know.... "

"Your call, but this is hostile country. I'm just figuring we can watch each other's back on the way."

"Reckon that sounds right. I'll side you." Shawnee pointed toward the hill in the background. "My camp's up yonder. I'll get my stuff and meet you back here."

"That'll give me time to find my pack mule. I lost him in the fracas back there."

Shawnee nodded and moved to his horse. He mounted and rode toward the area of his camp. Tell remounted and set out in the opposite direction, riding past the wounded man without a second look. When they both came together, Shawnee had broken camp, and Tell had found his pack mule. Shawnee's route changed, now heading southeast under Tell's directions.

They covered the three hundred odd miles to the vicinity of Fort Worth in two weeks. During the journey, though strictly guarding his own past from revelation, Shawnee became acquainted with Tell. For his part, Tell was forthcoming with his history as a pioneer and freedom-fighter during the Texas Republic's struggle for independence from Mexico, making him even more imposing to Shawnee than his mere height. Shawnee absorbed interesting facts about the background of Texas's break from Mexican rule as well as a cursory chronicle of Tell's life and battles and the establishment of the Tell Ranch as one of the largest enterprises in northeast Texas.

"When my wife died in childbirth, I decided I was going to build something substantial I could leave to my daughter. Now, she's got her future guaranteed, so when I pass, she's got no worries."

"Sounds like you been a good father to her."

"I surely tried. And she turned out real good. Wait'll you meet her."

Around a campfire one night about a week into the journey, Tell's curiosity got the better of him. "How'd you come by that name you use? It's not likely to be your given name."

"Meaning no disrespect, Mister Tell, but it's the name I use is all."

"I don't mean to pry, boy. Just idle curiosity. But, if somebody's on your trail, I can't help you if I don't know what to expect."

"I'm much obliged, sir, and for the offer as well. Let's just leave it at there's things in my recent past I'd just as leave keep there. Far as help's concerned, I've took care of myself pretty good so far. A job's all the help I'm after right now. If'n my past comes to call, I'll handle it. I won't involve you or yours."

"All right, Shawnee, we'll leave it at that for now. As long as you pull your weight and keep your nose clean, no questions asked. But, mind you, any sign of trouble, and you and I will have words. Time we got some shut-eye."

Shawnee smiled and nodded. They turned in for the night. The balance of the trip presented no further incidents.

The sun was high in the sky as they neared the Tell Ranch. Accustomed as he was to sparse living, Shawnee was flabbergasted by his first glimpse of the ranch complex. From a hill overlooking the spread, a huge main house faced south, a modified hacienda style building boasting two white pillars standing on either side of a hardwood double front door. In the background, a massive barn stood close to a barracks-type structure which Shawnee pegged to be the bunkhouse. Both were made of similar clapboard materials and in excellent states of maintenance. A large split-rail fence enclosed a corral system flanking the barn. Within its confines, two men in work clothing appeared to be training the several horses there with them, putting them through turning and stopping procedures.

"Well, there it is. Took me a lot of time, sweat, and blood to build it to what it is today. It's home to me and all who work it. It can be your home as well."

Shawnee was cautiously optimistic. It seemed too good to be true, but it was all he had. He reckoned he'd take it. "Mighty hospitable of you. I'll give it my best shot."

Tell led the way down the hill with Shawnee falling in behind the pack mule. They rode into the area and pulled up at the corral gate. Of the two men inside the corral, one, a black man, was mounted on one of the horses. He conducted what appeared to be maneuvers Shawnee guessed might be used to isolate steers from a herd. The second man, with a dark complexion, maybe Mexican, talked to another horse. Curiosity consumed Shawnee, but he held his tongue. If he was to know more about this, he would wait to be told.

Upon seeing Tell, the black man directed his mount to the corral gate where Tell and Shawnee waited.

"Howdy, Mister Tell, you and them others run them rustlers down, did you?" His voice was deep and resonant, squaring with his size.

"Nope, we came up dry, and I damn near got myself killed on the way back."

"Well, that ain't good."

This was the first time Shawnee even came close to a conversation with a Negro. Impressed with the man's confidence in speaking to his master, Shawnee studied the man. Blacker than Shawnee had seen before, the man's face was round and full, and he had a massive build on him. He sat straight in the saddle, not slumped and submissive like most slaves. Fascinated, Shawnee listened.

"I must be getting old, Cletus. I'm the best tracker in the bunch, and that's the only reason I ventured off with them, but we still couldn't turn up those jaspers. We wound up chasing the wind. On top of it all, I wandered right into an ambush on the way back. If it hadn't been for Shawnee, here, I'd have likely ended up dead and picked clean."

Cletus leaned forward in the saddle, showing great interest. "Sure glad he was there."

"I'll give you chapter and verse later. Right now, I need a meal and a bath. And I need to see Chrissie. She all right?"

Cletus grinned. "Yes, sir, right as rain."

Tell turned to Shawnee. "Shawnee, this is Cletus Workman, my foreman. Cletus, take this young man in tow, will you? He's coming to work for us. Need you to show him the ropes."

Cletus smiled. "I'll surely do that."

Tell dropped the reins of the pack mule and headed his mount toward the main house. Cletus moved closer to Shawnee. His eyes were on Shawnee, sizing him up, as Shawnee stared in disbelief at the fact a black man was the ranch foreman instead of just a slave.

"Not what you was expecting, am I?"

Uncertain how to react, Shawnee hesitated to answer.

"It's all right, I'm used to it." Cletus's smile continued as he spoke. "I ain't been a free man so long I done forgot how folks looks down on niggas."

"I... I wasn't—I didn't...."

"Sure you did. It's only natural. 'Special-like in these parts. But it don't work here. Not on the Tell. We all equal here, every man-jack of us. That's how Mister Tell made it. He don't care you're purple and you worship a prairie dog. Long as you pulls your weight and obeys the rules, you're welcome here. You get a clean place to sleep and three squares a day, and Mister Tell pays real good wages. Best in Texas, I'd say. So... is you and me going to have a problem over I be black and I be foreman and I gives the orders and you takes 'em?"

Shawnee considered, then answered up. "I reckon not."

"Well, that's real good. What's your name again?"

"Shawnee."

"Just the one name?"

"All's needed."

Cletus nodded knowingly. "Right. Shawnee it is. We all got things in our past. Don't matter here. Why don't you head on over to the bunkhouse there and drop your stuff. We'll get you squared away with a bunk and all later. Come on back, and we'll get you started. Plenty to do around here."

"Kind of wanted to try my hand at cowboying if you got a spot for me. I hear it to be a pretty good line of work."

"Good as any, I reckon." Cletus regarded Shawnee carefully. "You 'pears hefty enough. We can give it a try."

Shawnee smiled. "Thanks." He pulled Gray away from the corral and started toward the bunkhouse.

"Shawnee."

Shawnee stopped and turned to face Cletus.

"You won't be needing that sidearm for working. You can leave it with your stuff. It'll be safe enough."

"I got kind of partial to it of late. I'd just as leave keep it on if it's all the same to you."

Cletus shrugged. "No never-minds to me. It'll just get in your way is all, but your call."

Shawnee nodded and continued his ride toward the bunkhouse.

Walking back to the corral after dropping his belongings, Shawnee led Gray, intending to care for the horse inside the barn. As he moved, his thoughts wandered. He had not been called by his given name since he left Toby Joe and Kansas behind. For all intents and purposes, he was Shawnee now. This next step, signing on with the Tell Ranch, marked a new beginning. He would learn everything he could to excel at this job, and, for now at least, he would leave his past in Kansas. When the time was right to return, it wouldn't be Lon Pearce going back, it would be Shawnee, and he'd be ready.

He reached the corral gate to find Cletus back in the center of the area continuing his work with the horse he'd been instructing. The Mexican put another horse through several exercises, pivoting on front and hind legs, side-stepping, holding taut on a rope.

"Cletus." Shawnee's call was loud enough to be heard over the distance. "All right if I put my horse up? He's covered a lot of ground of late."

"Go ahead on," Cletus shouted back. "Come back with him when you're done. You start learning right off and him as well."

Shawnee did not pursue the question in his mind. What did "him as well" mean? He just nodded and went on to the barn.

TELL TRUDGED UP THE STEPS of the main house, his exhaustion slowing him. He'd left his horse tied to the hitch rail instead of putting the animal up as usual, another example of how tired he was. He'd need food and sleep, in that order, before he felt human again. Bath could come later. "Chrissie?"

"Pa, is that you?" The soft voice of his daughter brightened his spirits as he stepped into the parlor.

He hadn't a chance to answer when she burst in from another room. With an ear to ear grin, she hurried across the floor and grabbed him in a bear hug of an embrace. "You're home," she said into his chest. "I missed you." Her voice quivered as emotion took hold.

"And I missed you, girl." He wrapped his arms around her and lifted her off the floor for a second. Then he leaned back. "Let me look at you."

She was light complexioned with freckles on most of her face and light red hair, almost orange. It seemed a little wild, falling across her forehead in a pouf. Her face was round and had fine features, her mouth displaying what appeared to be a slight perpetual smile. His sixteen-year-old girl was turning into a fine young lady.

"I've only been gone a few weeks, and it seems you've grown again."

Chrissie became a little self-conscious. "I don't know. Maybe. Pa, are you all right? You seem real tired."

"Oh, I'm tired, yes, but I'm more frustrated than anything else. All that way and nothing to show for it. I'll be better when I get some good food and some rest in me."

"Then that's what we'll do. You go sit down, and I'll scare up some food for you. I know, I'll fry up some ham and eggs. I'm getting real good at it. I been practicing while you were gone."

Tell grinned. "Ham and eggs sounds just fine. I'll go set a spell."

After the meal, which Chrissie successfully prepared, they sat across from each other at the dining room table over remnants on their plates.

"You made 'em real good, girl. You're getting to be a first rate cook."

"As good as Cookie?" Chrissie's question referred to the ranch cook, one of the best of all the ranches in the area.

"I'd say you are."

Chrissie grinned. Then a sly expression crossed her face. "You know, Pa, there are a lot of other things I want to learn as well. When are you going to teach me to shoot? I want to learn that."

Tell smiled. "I know you do. Someday, Chrissie, someday. Sure won't be today though. I'm too tuckered."

"I know, but I so want to learn."

"Why, Chrissie? Why do you want to learn about guns?"

"So I can take care of myself if I ever have to. This is wild country. I want to feel safe."

"Good answer, but there's a lot of other things you'll need to learn. Day's coming pretty soon when you'll be going off to a school for young ladies so you can learn the finer points of lady-like living."

"Oh, I want to do that, too, Pa. I want to learn it all."

Tell got a faraway look in his eye. "There's going to come a time, sometime, when all this, the ranch and all, will be yours. I won't be around forever, you know. I want you to be ready for everything coming at you."

"And I will be. All the more reason for me to learn how to shoot."

Tell grinned. "You know what tenacious means?"

"I think it means persistent, doesn't it?"

"Yup, and that's exactly what you are, Chrissie Tell. Tenacious."

Chrissie smiled.

11

SHAWNEE REMOVED THE FEEDBAG FROM Gray's head. Man and horse stood in a stall about midway into the barn. Shawnee reached for two brushes from the floor.

"*Hola, amigo,*" the Mexican said from the entrance to the stall. He'd entered the barn quietly enough so as not to be noticed until he spoke.

He was half a head shorter than Shawnee but just as broad. With a dark complexion, his face had the shape of a muted triangle with a pronounced chin and a broad nose. He wore typical ranch work clothes with the addition of fringed buckskin shotgun chaps, leggings that fit snugly over pants.

"How do." Shawnee said pleasantly.

"I am Silvio Guzmán... Sil." His voice was even, his accent thick.

"Shawnee."

Sil nodded. "*Mucho gusto.* If you are done, we need you in the corral. Cletus will show you and I will show *su caballo...* your horse."

"Reckon I can brush him down later."

Sil picked up Gray's dangling reins. Instantly, the horse backed away and whinnied loudly, as if frightened. "*Oho.* A touchy one."

Shawnee had not seen Gray act this way before, but then no one had approached the horse in this manner since he owned him. This triggered a thought he'd had earlier about Gray's previous experiences. "Ain't seen him act that way before. Kind of makes me think the fellow owned him previous mistreated him. Here, I'll lead him out."

"No, *amigo*... he must allow this, or he don't learn."

Sil moved slowly forward, speaking quietly. "I don't hurt you, *muchacho*. Easy." He reached up to pet Gray's nose and face.

Shawnee sought to reassure Gray. "It's all right, Gray. He's all right."

The horse relaxed and responded favorably to Sil's advances, nodding its head and nickering. Sil led Gray out of the stall. Shawnee walked beside them. They proceeded to the corral where Cletus joined them. Sil took Gray into the center while Cletus worked with Shawnee near the fence.

"A good bit of cowboying gets did with a rope." As Cletus spoke, he lifted a well-worn coil of rope from a fence post. "Watch me close, then you try." Cletus stepped back about six feet and opened a wide loop, about the size of an average man, then twirled it over his head and dropped it over the post. As it settled in place, he drew it closed around the wood. He moved to the post and lifted the loop from it. After repeating the exercise several times, he recoiled the rope and handed it to Shawnee. "Now, you."

Shawnee took the rope and tried to duplicate Cletus's movements. He missed the post on the first two attempts but succeeded on the third. A smile crossed his face.

"Good." Cletus nodded. "Again."

Shawnee continued the exercise well into the afternoon until he became consistent and somewhat proficient. At the same time, Gray cooperated with Sil, learning by the touch of a crop which leg to use and which way to step, while constantly checking to make sure Shawnee was nearby. As the day wore on, the horse became comfortable with Sil's instructions and responded well to the lessons.

Shawnee and Cletus finished the rope work and approached the area where Sill still worked with Gray.

"This is one smart *caballo, amigo,*" Sil said to Shawnee. *"Míra."*

Sil moved closer to Gray. "Gray, *arríba.*" At the command, Gray reared sharply, leaning back on its rear hooves and flailing its front hooves in a mock attack. "Now, you try," Sil said as Gray settled down.

"What's that word you said?"

"Arríba. Means 'up.'"

"Uh-huh." Shawnee moved closer and duplicated Sil's command. Gray went through the same motions and quickly recovered. Shawnee went to Gray and gave the horse strokes around the head while speaking compliments in a low voice.

"Thanks, Sil. I reckon that might could come in handy sometime."

By the end of the day, both Shawnee and Gray were tired, but they had taken their first steps to becoming cowboy and cowpony.

Cletus walked with them toward the barn. "Tomorrow we'll head out to the herd. You can practice what you learned. I reckon you'll do all right. One more thing. You ain't met Mister Tell's daughter yet, but you will soon enough. Just make real certain you keeps your distance. Mister Tell tolerates most, but trust is altogether a different animal."

Shawnee shot a sideways glance at Cletus, feeling he was being accused. "I ain't the kind you're hinting at."

"Ain't saying you is. Just telling you, keep your distance."

After breakfast the next morning, Cletus, Sil, and Shawnee were joined by three other hands as they saddled up. As they led their horses out of the barn, Cletus spoke to Shawnee. "Make sure you got a bandana with you. New hands ride drag."

"What's drag?"

"You rides behind the herd and picks up strays. Wear the bandana over your nose to keep the dust out, less'n you likes choking."

Shawnee nodded. He resolved to deal with whatever he had to, to make this work.

They mounted and headed south toward the area where the herd grazed. As they rode, Shawnee's mind drifted back to Kansas, to his parents, to the sight of his father hanging from a tree, to his mother's body and her scrawl of the name of Teverence in the dirt beside her, to Teverence himself. He gritted his teeth at those awful memories and renewed his vow to someday take Teverence down, for good and all.

As they crested a hill, Shawnee got his first look at the herd. They milled around in a meadow, grazing. Although unable to estimate the number, he was confident in the fact it was more than he'd seen in one place before.

Cletus called a halt at the top of the hill and spoke to Shawnee. "We'll be heading them east about five miles to fresher grass. Ride in on them easy so's they don't spook." He led out down the slope at a slow pace and the others followed him.

After dismissing the crew already watching the herd, Cletus sent his group to their locations, himself at the front of the pack, two men on each side, and Shawnee at the rear. At Cletus's call, the hands shouted out and swung their ropes to get the cattle moving. Shawnee quickly learned what Cletus meant about riding drag as he tied his bandana around his neck and pulled it up over his nose. Trail dust from the herd's hooves swirled and raised around him, settling on his clothes and hat. While the bandana provided some protection, he expected he'd be tasting dust for days to come.

About a mile into the drive, Sil left his post on the side of the herd to join Shawnee. Sil said nothing. He simply fell in alongside Shawnee and waved his hand in a sort of haphazard salute. Shawnee nodded in appreciation for the companionship as Sil pulled his bandana over his nose.

Halfway through the trip, a calf, lagging behind the herd, wandered off. Shawnee caught sight of the little one and turned Gray to chase it down. As they approached the errant calf, Shawnee swung his rope and let the loop fly. His throw missed as the calf changed direction and scurried away. Shawnee followed, putting Gray into a gallop, and stood in the stirrups to steady himself as he swung another loop. This time, the rope dropped around the calf's neck. Shawnee pulled Gray up sharply, yanking the calf off its legs. He waited for the animal to get up, then led it, squalling and tugging, back to the herd. When he was close to the cattle, he stopped and dismounted. Gray held the rope taut. Shawnee walked the rope back to the struggling calf, released the bawling youngster, and shooed it back into the herd. With everything under control, Shawnee remounted and rejoined Sil on drag, coiling up the rope as he rode.

"*Bueno.* You did well, *amigo.*"

"Thanks." The smile on Shawnee's face was not visible through the bandana. He did, however, seem to sit taller in the saddle.

The trip only consumed a few hours. When the group arrived at the east range, they drove the cattle into a lush meadow with fresh grass and a natural basin to keep the herd restrained. Shortly after their arrival, the chuck wagon showed up, and the cook proceeded to set up for lunch. After the meal, Cletus gave the hands their assignments. Shawnee ended up with nighthawk duty, another undesirable task typically given to new hands.

"You patrols the beeves at night and keeps them from roaming off. Talk to 'em, sing to 'em, I don't care how you does it. Just keep 'em together. So, you might want to get some shut-eye now. You'll be up all night."

Shawnee took the advice and set his bedroll out a short distance from the camp. He slept while the rest of the crew tended the herd. A short time later, he was awakened by the cook's call for supper. After the meal, Shawnee saddled Gray and set about his duties.

Darkness fell as he relieved the hands who had not yet eaten. He found himself alone to ride the perimeter and keep stragglers bunched in with the herd. Speaking quietly to the cattle seemed to keep them settled down. When he tired of speaking, Shawnee began humming a nondescript tune, even putting some words to it, though they made no sense. Amazingly, the animals responded well to his song, so he continued. They did not seem to mind his off-key singing. Good thing they didn't know better.

Further into the night, Shawnee's thoughts wandered back to Kansas and his promise to seek revenge on Teverence. This stayed with him throughout his shift, which served to keep him awake until his relief took over in the morning

The same routine went on for about a week until a fresh crew arrived to take over from Cletus's men. Cletus put one of the new arrivals in charge and led his crew back to the ranch area.

"Take the rest of the day off," Cletus told them. "Come morning, we got us some clean up to do."

"All right if I get in some target practice? Don't want to get rusty."

"Ain't no never-minds to me. Just see you take it out back a the barn."

Shawnee went to the trash bin outside the cook shack, gathering an armful of empty food tins. He took them to a spot a few yards behind the barn and set them on the ground in a horizontal row. Walking about twenty feet back toward the barn, he turned sharply while drawing his sidearm, firing five shots in rapid succession, aiming carefully. The dull, loud report of the Navy Colt echoed across the plains as he viewed the result through rising gunsmoke. Four of the five cans had been hit. The last one still remained in place. He shook his head, unsatisfied.

"That was amazing." The soft female voice behind him snatched his attention. He turned to see a slim, delicate looking girl standing at the corner of the barn wall. Shawnee guessed her age to be close to his own, maybe a year or two younger. He reckoned she'd be Tell's daughter.

Finding himself gawking at her, he finally forced himself to recover. "Nah! That's just average."

She took a few steps closer and stood with her hands clasped behind her back. "Looked good to me. I'm Chrissie."

He tugged at his hat. "How do. Shawnee."

"You're new here, aren't you?"

"A few days, yes, ma'am."

She moved closer. He watched her, observing her yellow, flowered dress as it flowed with her movements, accentuating her figure. He guessed it was expensive, reflecting the wealth Bruno Tell appeared to possess. Then he saw her eyes, big and wide, the softest sky blue color he'd ever seen.

"I'm not a ma'am." Her correction was gentle. "Call me Chrissie."

"Yes, ma'am." It came out before he could stop it, and they both chuckled at his verbal stumble. "I mean... Miss Chrissie."

"That's better. Would you show me how to shoot?"

The girl's question was matter-of-fact. It caught him unawares, and her directness caused him to hesitate. "Well... I don't know. You ever shot a gun before?"

"No, but I want to learn. My pa never seems to have time for it."

Shawnee pondered for a few seconds. "Reckon it can't hurt none." He definitely knew the basics and how to teach them since they were still fresh in his mind from the instruction Toby Joe had provided. The prospect of spending time with this girl and getting much closer to her made this more attractive than a cut-and-dried practice session. "Let me reload, and I'll show you."

"Thank you."

She came even closer to watch him reload the revolver, again with her hands behind her. Shawnee already felt a bit awkward. This new nearness made him more nervous than he expected, to the point of fumbling the process. He overloaded powder into one of the chambers and had to dump it and begin again. Then he dropped one of the balls as he tried lining it up with the chamber. This caused him to flash a self-conscious grin at her. She reciprocated and continued to watch. Finally, taking twice as long as it should, he finished loading. At the same time, he became aware of a flushed feeling throughout his body. He hoped this didn't show in his face.

Holstering the Colt, Shawnee placed Chrissie in the spot from which he had fired, touching her arms gingerly. He put the gun in her hand. "Don't touch the trigger till you're ready to shoot. Keep your trigger finger straight out under the cylinder here. Aim at one of the tins and focus your eyes on the front sight. Put the sight right under what you're shooting at and right in the V notch in the hammer there." He allowed her time to get comfortable with what he'd shown her before going on.

"It's heavy." She giggled.

"Reckon it is, but you get used to it after a spell. Now, when you shoot, the gun's going to kick. It'll go up and back into your arm. Bend your arm a little and lock it in place. Lean into the gun. If you don't, it'll knock you over."

She adjusted her stance.

"That's good. Now, with your left thumb, pull the hammer all the way back till it stops. Then aim and put your finger on the trigger and ease it straight back. Steady press it."

Chrissie followed his instructions. He put his hand on her back as a support should the recoil be too much for her. The gun fired, its soft report resounding around them. A chinking sound could be heard at the same time. At the same instant, the barrel came up sharply and forced her arm back into her shoulder. Her back pushed against his hand, but he held her there. She stood there, surprised. Black powder smoke clouded the area.

The smoke cleared to allow a view of the targets. "You hit it!"

She looked to see the tin, displaced by about a foot.

"I hit it!" There was glee in her voice as he reached the revolver out of her hand. Turning to him with the broadest grin he had ever seen, she repeated, "I hit it!" with even more joy than the first time.

Shawnee smiled. "Now, don't get too confident. But, I got to say, if you can hit a tin can, you can surely hit a... I mean... you can—"

"I want to do it again." She sounded like a child with a new toy.

He was glad she cut him off because he didn't want to finish what had started coming out. "All right."

She turned to face the targets as he placed the gun in her hand. Duplicating her original movements, she fired again but missed.

"It don't always work. Try again."

She did, and the tin chinked and bounced away. As she turned to face Shawnee, something behind him caught her attention, and her expression changed to one of concern.

The voice coming from there was familiar. "What's all this?"

Shawnee turned as Cletus stepped out from the corner of the barn and moved toward them. "What's going on here?"

Chrissie spoke up. "Shawnee's showing me how to shoot. I hit two out of three."

Cletus stopped close to Shawnee and trained his eyes on him as he spoke to Chrissie. "Miss Chrissie, you knows how your pa feels about these here things. You'd best head back to the house now. I need to have some words with Shawnee."

Chrissie did not readily move.

"Miss Chrissie." Cletus hardened his voice. "I think it best you goes... right now."

She reluctantly stepped around them, handed the gun back to Shawnee, and walked away.

Shawnee faced Cletus, saying nothing, as Cletus glared at him. He holstered the Colt.

Cletus studied him for a long moment, cocking his head to the side very slightly. "Let me ask you something. What part of 'keep your distance' from her didn't come out clear to you?"

"Reckon I forgot is all."

"You 'membered everything else, your roping and all, but you forgot that part, eh? Well, you know what? I don't buy it." As he spoke, Cletus jabbed Shawnee's chest with his index finger. "I think you decided you'd just go ahead on and take up with her 'cause she's pretty and all."

The finger stabbing continued.

Shawnee stared back at Cletus. "Don't poke me." His voice was low and warning.

"I'll poke you to make a point if'n I got a mind to." And he poked Shawnee again.

"I *said* don't poke me."

"Young'un, I'm the boss here. I tell you do something, you damn well better do it, or they be hell to pay."

Shawnee's voice went up an octave. "Cletus, I'm telling you, don't poke me no more."

"I'll poke you. I'll do whatever it take to make you tow. You get that?"

"Cletus, I'm telling you—"

"What you telling me?" Cletus shouted. He poked again. "You telling me you ain't following orders? You just doing what you want? I'll kick your ass off this place if that's what you telling me."

"I'm telling you stop poking me."

Cletus poked him again.

"Son of a bitch." Shawnee hauled back and swung a wide right at Cletus. The other man's left arm came up to block the swing, and, at the same time, he shot a short right jab, catching Shawnee's chin, shoving his head straight back and moving his body backwards a few inches. The surprised expression on Shawnee's face betrayed his reaction to the blow. It did not settle this, however. Shawnee's expression was intense as he swung his left to find it blocked as well. This time Cletus's return was a left hook that smacked Shawnee's jaw and sent him to the ground. He felt the pain from both blows as a fuzziness crept into his head.

"Stay down!"

Shawnee looked up to see Cletus now in a fight-ready stance, left extended, right tucked to his chest.

Determined to prevail, Shawnee scrambled to his feet and tried to duplicate Cletus's position. He stepped forward into an attempted right cross. Cletus was quicker, landing two fast left jabs and a short right. Shawnee was dumped back on the ground.

"I said stay down."

Now groggy and hurting about the face, Shawnee rolled to his side and attempted to get up, but he could find neither the strength nor clarity to do so. He peered up at Cletus towering over him. "Reckon I'll stay down."

"Good choice. You about ready to follow all the rules?"

"Yeah."

"Fair enough." Cletus reached out a hand to help Shawnee to his feet. "Now, you keeps your distance from Miss Chrissie, and you do your job best you can, and we're good. Don't none of this need to go beyond here."

"All right." Shawnee pulled off his bandana to mop whatever

blood might have been on his face. He felt welts beginning to form where Cletus's fists connected.

"Get yourself cleaned up." Cletus turned away to leave.

"Cletus."

"Uh-huh." Cletus turned to face him.

"I'd be obliged you'd show me how to do that."

"Do what?"

"Fight with my hands like you do."

Cletus cracked a slight smile. "Tell you what, you learn me to shoot, and I'll learn you to fight. Do we gots a deal?"

Shawnee smiled back, "That sounds real good."

12

THE NEXT YEAR WAS EVENTFUL in Shawnee's new life as a cowhand. Filled with activity, each day was a learning experience for him. He put in his share of nighthawk duty, chased down strays, pulled steers from water holes and bogs, dodged angry bulls when he got too close to their cows, and put Gray through paces he thought impossible. Gradually, under the tutelage of Cletus and Sil, he developed into a top hand, surpassing the accomplishments of older, more experienced workers. His ability to ride, cut steers from the herd, rope and brand, and all the minor duties associated with working cattle grew quickly.

Sil brought him to Fort Worth on a supply run, and, there, he found a store which offered everything he needed. Gradually, as he was able to afford them, he replaced his farm clothes with the outfit of a cowhand—boots, hat, canvas pants as well as cutting chaps to protect his lower body from thick bushes and the horns of steers.

In his off hours, Shawnee taught Cletus to shoot, employing all the lessons and tricks Toby Joe had imparted. And Cletus reciprocated, instructing Shawnee in the fine art of fisticuffs.

"Hitting ain't about losing your temper. It's about sizing up who you're up against. How big is he? How fast is he? Watch his eyes.

They'll tell you when he's going to move 'fore he moves. You figure out what he's going to do and you do to him before he can do to you. Don't hold back like I done with you. Take him down fast-like, 'fore he knows what hit him."

When Cletus could shoot as well as Shawnee, and Shawnee could knock Cletus down with several well placed punches, they decided they had gone far enough. The two men, along with Sil, became a working team as well as developing a close friendship. In addition to almost guessing the others' moves, they hunted together in their off hours.

During this time, Shawnee followed the rules regarding Chrissie, keeping his distance, limiting his interactions with her to pleasant greetings. He had a definite attraction to her, but pursuing a relationship with her would not work out well for either of them. A wanted man with no future prospects other than killing or being killed had no business taking on the responsibility of a woman. Maybe she had feelings for him, but he kept out of her way by staying busy and even intentionally avoiding her in the hope it would not develop further.

The entire crew returned from the range after completing the fall roundup and branding. Bruno Tell approached Shawnee as he unsaddled Gray in the barn.

"Shawnee."

"Yes, sir."

"Cletus tells me you've been showing him how to shoot. Says you're the best gun handler he's ever seen."

"Well, I get by."

"You do more'n just get by to hear him tell it. Look, Chrissie's been after me over a year now to teach her to shoot. I put it off as long as I could, but I think it's time she learned. I'd like you to teach her."

The request confused Shawnee. He hesitated to reply for a noticeable amount of time.

"Something bothering you, boy?"

"Truth be told, there is. Last year, Chrissie asked me to show her shooting, and I did some. But Cletus saw us and dressed me down for overstepping. Told me to keep my distance from her. Now, you're asking the exact opposite of me. Reckon I'm a tad perplexed by the whole thing now."

"Understandable." Tell nodded slowly. "See, Cletus feels beholden to me 'cause I bought him out of slavery and gave him his freedom. There's not a thing he won't do for me and mine, and he protects Chrissie like she's his own. If you're worried about running afoul of him, don't. I'll talk to him."

"Already crossed that line, but we settled it."

Tell nodded slowly. "Not something I need to know about. Cletus aside, will you teach her? She's driving me up a tree over this."

"Reckon I can show her. Ask her to meet me back of the barn after supper tonight."

Tell shook Shawnee's hand. "I'll owe you one for this, so anything I can do for you, just let me know."

Shawnee thought for a second. His mind drifted back to the day he arrived at the ranch. "Well, sir, there might could be something."

Tell studied him. "What's on your mind?"

"Day you done brought me here, you was going on about how you be a good tracker and all. I'd surely like to learn the how of that if you would."

Tell smiled. "Yeah, tracking's always a good skill for you to know. I'll arrange it." He walked away leaving Shawnee raising his hat and scratching his head, still taken aback by the Chrissie conundrum.

After the evening meal, Shawnee ambled out behind the barn with an armful of empty tins. He set up the target line and fired five rounds to loosen up, scoring five out of five. As he reloaded the Colt,

Chrissie rounded the corner of the barn and approached. He looked up from the gun. "Evening, Miss Chrissie."

Her smile turned to a frown. "I wish you'd stop calling me 'miss.' It makes me sound like an old spinster."

"Not my intention." He tried to watch his words to keep from saying something she might take the wrong way, like a compliment. This caused him to almost trip over his next question. "How you want I should I say it?"

"Just Chrissie. Please."

"Chrissie it is. You ready?"

"I am." Her smile returned.

He finished loading the gun and handed it to her, butt first.

"Can I wear the holster so I can learn to draw?"

Shawnee checked her over for size. "Well, now, fellow give me this rig was a tad wider'n me. Me being wider'n you, I don't reckon there's holes enough for it to work on you. Tell you what, you find yourself a belt that fits you, and we can slip the holster on it real easy. We can do it for next time."

"All right. Next time." She took the revolver and turned to the targets.

He watched her pull the hammer back. "Remember. Focus on the front site."

Chrissie's first shot missed. Shawnee, standing behind her, suggested sighting on the target and then bringing the gun up into the sight picture, forcing her eye to see the front sight. He taught her trigger control, explaining she should press the trigger straight back without moving the gun. The next shot hit the can. At the end of the session, she not only had the ability to hit everything she aimed at but picked up the skill of loading the weapon.

"When can we do this again?" A broad grin accompanied her question as Shawnee holstered the Colt.

"I'm going out to the herd in the morning. I'll come get you when I get back. Couple or three days, I reckon." He walked her to the main house and tipped his hat. "Night, Chrissie."

Chrissie smiled coyly. "Good night, Shawnee. Thank you."

Shawnee nodded. "Yup."

He returned from his range duties three days later. The next morning, he went to the ranch house and asked Tell to send Chrissie out to meet him. She appeared this time wearing a plum colored polka dot blouse and a dark skirt with a leather belt. "Good morning, Shawnee. Will this do?" She indicated the belt as she spoke.

He observed as she stepped into the increasing sunlight. She was surely a vision. Careful now. "I reckon so. Let's go try it out."

They stepped off the porch and walked to the spot behind the barn.

"Was it hard work?" Chrissie asked, obviously trying to start a conversation.

"How's that?"

"The time you spent with the herd, was it hard?"

Shawnee shrugged. "Well, you know, it's the job. You do what you have to."

"Do you like it?"

"Some. I like it better'n farming. Farming's boring. Leastwise, cowboying, you change it up now and again."

They reached the shooting spot. Shawnee slipped the holster off his gun belt, lifted the gun out, and held the holster out to her. She loosed her belt and slipped it on.

"I missed shooting while you were gone." She buckled the belt.

"Well... I missed learning you."

"Did you? Really?" Her coyness became more apparent as she smiled and stroked an errant hair away from her face.

"Well, sure." He tried to recover from this big gopher hole he'd just stepped in. "It's rewarding seeing you shoot good, knowing it's my doing."

"Is that the only reason?"

Shawnee stopped dead, saying nothing, his mouth partially open. There was the gopher hole again. He cleared his throat. "Reckon we better get to shooting."

"Shawnee?"

"Now, Chrissie, you look-a-here. We come out here to learn shooting. Now, I don't know what you're about, but, if it ain't about shooting, we got no business getting into it."

"I just wanted to know if it's the only reason."

Shawnee decided it was time to clear the air. "Truth be told, no, no it ain't. I like you, Chrissie, like you a lot, but we can't be doing that. You don't know nothing 'bout me, 'cepting I'm a stranger happens to work here and happens to know about guns. If you're aiming for this to be more, well, it can't be. Ain't fair to neither of us. Now, I'm willing to show you shooting like you want and be a friend to you, but that's got to be the all of it."

A pouting expression crossed her face. "But you said you like me."

"Like a friend, Chrissie, only like a friend. I ain't got the wherewithal for it to be no more'n friendly-like."

"Oh...."

Watching her face form a frown, he felt the need to apologize. "Aw, Chrissie, I'm sorry. This was a bad idea from the get-go. I should have said no when your pa asked me... even before when you asked me. Maybe we ought to just... I don't know... forget the whole thing."

She recovered immediately. "No. We can still do this. We can still be friends."

Shawnee hesitated for a second. "Long as friends is the all of it."

Chrissie relented. "Yes, Shawnee." She sighed. "That'll be the all of it."

He let it go then. "All right, then, let's get to shooting."

IN THE YEAR THAT FOLLOWED, Shawnee continued to learn and develop as a reliable worker and a dependable friend. His bond with Cletus and Sil solidified. They had become an inseparable team. His relationship with Chrissie remained a friendship, mostly because, when he was not instructing her, he stayed clear of her. He managed to find work to do or reasons to be away from the main area. It was not long before Chrissie realized her overtures would not show the results she desired. She eventually backed off.

During this period, Shawnee met regularly with Bruno Tell on the range. True to his word, Tell taught Shawnee the finer points of tracking, how to distinguish between the hoof print of a cow and a horse, how to determine if a horse's prints were made by a white rider or an Indian. "Indians don't shoe their horses." He pointed out the subtle differences in size and shape between horses' hooves, so a tracker could zero in on following an individual rider, even if the rider was part of a group. "Besides just following a trail, a tracker's got to see the bigger picture of where his subject is going. If it's one man, scanning the country in front of you can pick out little spots where he could be hiding in ambush, so you don't bull straight on in. You kind of skirt around to see if you can spot him before he spots you. If it's a group, being able to see where the group can fit up ahead and where it can't can tell you more than just following tracks. You learn tracking by doing, so we'll be repeating this often, till you get to where you get a sixth sense about it. Then you'll be ready."

Shawnee proved an apt pupil, displaying an innate affinity for the subject. After several lessons lasting a few days each, he was able to solve tracking problems Tell had set up without help. He was ready.

Besides the new skill, Shawnee learned a new respect for Tell. He already knew the man was a good parent to Chrissie, but he began to look on Tell with the same esteem he held for his father. Their developing relationship formed a bond that kept Seth alive in Shawnee's mind. Someday he'd go back....

———

IN THE BEGINNING OF MAY 1865, Tell returned from a trip to Fort Worth with news significant enough for him to call all the hands together for a meeting, even sending Sil out to summon those working the ranges. As the group gathered in front of the main house porch, Tell stepped out to face them with Chrissie at his side.

"Men, I've got important news. The war is over. General Lee surrendered to the Union Army last month."

Loud discussion followed. Since this crew came from both North and South, arguments displayed mixed feelings about which side deserved to win the war. Varied loyalties which had been suspended during their time at The Tell now came to the surface. Tell called for quiet.

"When this war started, I wanted no part of it. That's why I created a separate world, here on The Tell. I opened it up to all who believed, like I do, they wanted no part of this conflict. I took in anyone who had a past they weren't proud of, who needed a place where no pursuers could reach them, who just wanted to be left alone to live their lives. All I asked in return was loyalty to the Tell brand, and you've given that, over and over again.

"Well, now we're at a crossroads. I know there are a lot of you who have families you want to get back to, who'll no longer need this place as a haven. So, anyone who needs to leave has my blessing and my thanks for making The Tell what it is today. But, at the same time, this is a business. The end of the war means there won't be a Confederate army to buy our beef. We'll have to find new markets, and, I can tell you right now, they will not be in Texas. Not for the short term anyway. The only way we can survive is to drive the herds north for sale. To do that, I'll need hands, a lot of them. If you're with me, step up and welcome. If you need to leave, I savvy and no hard feelings, but I need to know it right now, so I know how many are staying and how many I have to replace. So, take a minute, right now, and decide."

The discussion began again, louder this time. Shawnee, Cletus, and Sil spent no time at all deciding. As others continued to debate, they stepped forward, creating distance between them and the group. In moments, others moved forward to join them until the ones committing to stay outnumbered by half again those choosing to leave or who were still in the process of deciding.

Looking the group over, Tell grinned. "Better than I expected."

Cletus glanced over his shoulder at those now choosing to leave. "About what I thought."

Tell stepped down off the porch and stood in front of Cletus. "I want you to get a roundup going. I want the whole herd ready to move at a minute's notice."

Cletus took his men in tow and began assigning hands to various locations with orders to roundup and brand every head in the Tell herd. While this went on, Tell went to those who were not staying.

"You men'll be paid to the end of the week," he told them. "You can leave then. I thank you for all you've done, and I wish you good fortune."

Several men stepped up and shook his hand, thanking him for his help and council. Slowly, they all left the area.

OVER THE COURSE OF THE next two weeks, the crew went through a complete roundup as well as the branding of those animals born after the last gathering had taken place. The cowboys worked hard to make the herd ready for the trail. At the same time, Tell conducted communications with cattle buyers in the north and finally settled on a deal to deliver three to four thousand head to Abilene, Kansas, come August. When word got around about the drive, several smaller ranchers in the area requested Tell incorporate their herds with his own. He agreed, which called for additional roundups and branding operations.

When he learned the destination of the drive was Kansas, Shawnee saw the possibility of getting closer to his ultimate goal of killing Teverence. He planned to work the drive to its completion, then leave and make his way back to confront his enemy.

Toward the end of May, Tell held a meeting in the bunkhouse with Cletus and the top hands.

"Now that the other herds are mixed in with ours, it's time to start a drive north. My deal with the broker calls for delivery in Abilene no later than August fifteenth. Gives you two months to get there. Can you do it?"

"We'll do 'er." Cletus said confidently.

"Good man. Take as many men as you'll need. The rest will stay behind to work the ranch, but you'll have to leave someone you trust to oversee them. Your choice."

Cletus thought for a moment. "Shawnee can handle it. He ready."

In that instant, Shawnee saw his plan of revenge crumbling. If he accepted the proposal, he would likely have to wait until the following year to head for Kansas, but, if he accompanied the drive, the wait to get to Kansas would be shortened by months. His desire to deal with Teverence, while always an underlying wish, now became essential. He needed a reason to refuse, and he pushed his mind to create one.

"Hold on, Cletus. I should go with the drive. I can help, what with the tracking skills Mister Tell learned me. 'Sides, I skirted around Abilene on my way down to Texas. I might could find us a way there."

Cletus considered. "You got a point there. We'll need all the help we can get. You ride scout for the drive. I'll figure somebody else to stay back."

Shawnee grinned. "Proud to."

"How soon can you start?" Tell asked.

Cletus answered up. "Herd's ready. We can head out in the morning."

"See me before you leave. I'll have money for you to take with you for expenses on the trail and to pay the crew when you get to Abilene." Tell placed a hand on Cletus's shoulder. "I hope you know I'm trusting you with the future of all of us."

"We won't let you down, Mister Tell."

Tell nodded and said no more. He left the bunkhouse.

Cletus assigned duties to each man. He turned to Sil. "I need you to work the remuda back of the drive, Sil. Don't take it as a step-down. Ain't nobody as good with horses as you be."

The *remuda* was the collection of spare horses trailing the herd. They supplied back-up mounts to keep the hands working. This position was usually occupied by a young, inexperienced wrangler.

"Está bien, amigo, I do it."

Shawnee was gratified, to some degree at least, the trio would be together for the drive.

Early the next morning, the crew prepared to leave. Chrissie made her way from the main house toward the corral fence where Shawnee tightened the cinch on Gray's saddle. She called him as she approached. He turned toward her.

"I wanted to say goodbye," she said as she reached him. She stood close to him.

"Surely mighty nice of you, Chrissie, coming out this early and all."

Concern crossed her face. "You're coming back, aren't you?"

"Well, I can't promise nothing. Never know what's going to happen."

"I want you to come back." Before he had chance to reply, she reached up, threw her arms around his neck, and kissed him on the lips.

Surprised, he stood there. In truth, he enjoyed the kiss, his first ever, but it stunned him.

Her face was red. She let go of him, spun around, took off, and trotted back toward the house. "Goodbye."

Shawnee's hand went to the back of his neck. "Bye."

13

HAVING LAGGED BEHIND WHILE HE recovered from Chrissie's kiss, Shawnee galloped Gray to the area where the huge herd grazed. He pulled up sharply alongside Cletus at the front of the herd. Cletus had already placed his crew at strategic points throughout the pack. Sil tended the remuda of a dozen horses off to the side of the herd.

Cletus flashed a grin. "You all goodbyed out, are you?"

"How do you figure?"

"When you going to learn there ain't much goes on I misses?"

Shawnee grinned. "I reckon."

"All right, then. You ride point with me till we run out of country we knows the lay of. Then you go ahead on and scout us a trail."

Shawnee nodded.

Cletus turned in his saddle, took off his hat, and waved it forward. "Head 'em north!"

At the call, the crew shouted and swung ropes to get the cattle moving. They started slowly and then gathered momentum. Dust rose from their many hooves and joined the light breeze of the morning. The gentle wind carried it off to the east as the sound of the cattle moving mimicked steady soft thunder.

Cletus and Shawnee struck out at a canter to lead the herd and to set the pace. As the last steers passed, Sil held the remuda in check to allow the dust to clear, then he started the horses to follow the steers. It was a smooth beginning to a five-hundred-mile journey.

For the first week on the trail, the drive averaged about ten miles per day. They bedded the cattle down at night. During this time, the hands became accustomed to spending each day moving the cattle. Cletus cautioned them early on. He'd enforce the rules, and he was the ultimate authority for the duration of the drive. "Any trouble twixt any of you, keep it off the trail. You can settle it in camp, away from the beeves. I catch any man with a bottle, he gone in a minute. No pay and no second chances. We'll get along just fine without you. You got a problem with any of what I just said, you can ride out now."

No one left. No one drank, and the few quarrels that arose, dumb things like who was first in the chow line, were hashed out in private, at night, without guns. They knew better than to run afoul of Cletus.

After several weeks of rolling north, the group approached unfamiliar ground, the end of the flat Texas plains and the beginning of Oklahoma hill country.

In camp, Cletus took Shawnee aside after an evening meal. "According to my map, if we keep heading north, we runs right into Indian Territory, but, if we head northwest, we got to cross the Cherokee Outlet. I hear that's outlaw country. So what do you reckon we do?"

"There's no law in the Outlet. They just run free. At least, Indian Territory's got government control. Outlaws aside, if we head northwest, we'll likely add a couple weeks to the trip. I say we cut straight north across Indian Territory and take our chances."

"Can you scout us a way through?"

"I got myself across Kansas without help 'fore I met up with Mister Tell. I reckon I can."

"All right, then. Head out in the morning. Scout what you can each day and head back to camp by nightfall to report. Keep a sharp eye out."

"Don't worry, I will." Shawnee turned to leave.

"Shawnee."

He looked around at the call.

"You be on your own out there. I can't spare men to go after you case you don't make it back."

"Won't be the first time."

"See it ain't your last."

Shawnee nodded and left to bed down for the night. In the morning, he packed provisions into his saddlebags and saddled Gray for the trail.

Sil approached on foot as Shawnee mounted up. "Hey, *amigo, cuidádo, eh?*"

"I will." Shawnee started Gray moving. He rode to the edge of camp at a walk, then increased speed as they moved away.

Over the next four days, he found trails north into Indian Territory large enough to accommodate the herd, returning each night to deliver the route to Cletus.

With the drive about forty miles into the Indian Territory, he set out on the fifth day. It was still morning when he crested a hill and stopped to examine the lay of the land. The crack of a rifle echoed from the distance to his right. Putting Gray into an immediate gallop, he headed straight for an outcropping of rocks about an eighth of a mile forward and to his left. As he reached them, he pulled the Henry from its scabbard and slipped out of the saddle. The rock he chose for cover was big enough to shield both him and Gray. He propped his body against the stone and waited, scanning the horizon for signs of an adversary. Nothing.

Unwilling to waste time sitting behind a rock, Shawnee decided to push the situation to determine if he was the target of the shot or if he had reacted without cause. As he raised his head above cover, a bullet pinged off the stone not a foot from him. A split second later, the report resounded from the same general location as the first. He had his answer, and now he could be pinned down here all day if he allowed it.

Needing to draw the shooter out, he settled on a game of playing possum. He scanned the area behind him and found a pocket in the rocks he could hide behind. Satisfied with his plan, he removed his hat and raised it just above the rock surface to mimic a man walking. Then he placed the hat in plain sight on the top of the boulder and dropped below the spot.

Within seconds, a bullet ripped the hat away. The sound echoed again through the hills. Next he would spring the trap. Shawnee stayed below the top of the boulder and made his way to the hiding spot. Settling in behind it, he waited, the Henry at port arms, poised for action.

Several tense minutes passed. With virtually no wind, the quiet was deafening. Then, in the distance, Shawnee heard the hoof beats of one horse approaching. The sound told him the horse wasn't shod, one of the tidbits he'd learned from Tell's tracking lessons. The noise stopped just shy of the rock formation. He could now hear the scuffling of padded feet moving forward. He waited.

The shooter defiantly entered the spot where he expected a body to be. When the footsteps stopped, Shawnee had his cue to act. He stepped clear of his hiding spot to see a man in buckskins and moccasins standing over the plugged hat, a bewildered expression on his dark red face.

"Hey!" Shawnee shouted as the Henry came to his shoulder. Startled, the man looked up and tried to bring his rifle to bear. Shawnee's shot went dead center, penetrating the chest, knocking the body back a few inches before sprawling the man on the ground.

Shawnee kept his rifle ready and moved slowly forward to examine the result. This was the first hostile Indian he had ever encountered. Sure, he had seen redskins before, hanging around idly in towns now and again, but never up close, never armed, never dangerous. He crouched to a knee to check for life. There was no breathing, just the open mouthed, surprised expression on the dead man's face. He rose and scanned the area forward of the rock formation for any sign of additional predators. He saw no one.

Picking up his hat, Shawnee went to Gray and led the horse back onto the trail, passing the body unceremoniously. There he mounted and set out for the general location from which the dead Indian had emerged, scrutinizing the land for anything out of place.

It was not long before he found the man's shooting spot, given away by the three spent shell casings strewn on the ground. It was another outcropping of rocks on the other side of the trail and it led to a path through the formation to a natural rim above an arroyo. A chanting sound rose from below the rim. He pulled Gray up and dismounted. He waved his hand toward the ground. "Gray, wait." He moved on to the rim.

Peering down, Shawnee saw the reason for the attack. He viewed on the arroyo floor a group of Indians dressed in the same manner as the dead man. They numbered in the dozens and seemed to be going through some kind of ritual dance. The dead man likely was a sentry charged with keeping away unwanted visitors. This told him their ceremony was not of a friendly nature. Some of their gyrations involved brandishing their bows and rifles in a threatening way. Shit! What did he stumble onto?

The chanting became more pronounced, the movements of the Indians more agitated, as if they were working themselves up, preparing for some confrontation. Shawnee thought it best to go back and warn the drive to hold up until he could find a way around these jaspers.

Returning to Gray, Shawnee mounted and made his way through the pass and back to the trail. Then he put Gray into a full gallop and did not let up until the dust from the drive came into his view. Heading straight for the herd, he took the chance his aggressive movements might spook the steers. He closed in on Cletus.

"Cletus! Hold up! Hold 'em up!" His shouts put Cletus into action. He signaled to the crew to halt the herd. Shawnee pulled up sharply in front of Cletus, out of breath.

"What's going on?" Cletus asked as Shawnee settled Gray.

"Spotted a band of Injuns in a gulch north of here. They was going through some kind of... I don't know... war dance, maybe. They surely ain't acting friendly. One of them tried to kill me when I come on 'em. Reckon you should ought to hold the herd here. I'll see if I can find a way to skirt around them."

Cletus looked around, somewhat frantically. "They come at us, we're no good in the open like this. We got to get to where we can hold the herd."

"I passed a box canyon maybe a mile back from here. Reckon it'd be big enough to fit the herd. I'll lead you back there and—"

"Hey! What's that coming?" The call came from a cowboy working the side of the herd. He pointed to a dust cloud rising in the east about a mile out.

Shawnee and Cletus focused on it. Shawnee squinted to see better. "Might be them."

"We can't chance it ain't. Head for the canyon. We'll follow."

Shawnee spun Gray in place and set out for the box canyon as Cletus shouted to the hands to start the herd to safety. "Stampede 'em if you got to, but keep 'em bunched up! Follow Shawnee!" As the cattle passed him, Cletus headed back to the location of the chuck wagon and Sil with the remuda. "We got Injuns coming on. Catch the herd up."

The ride to the box canyon was short and hard. Shawnee pulled Gray to a stop and turned to see the herd moving fast straight for him. He rode to the side of the canyon entrance and waited. The crew drove the cattle into the canyon and then formed a line at the entrance to prevent the herd from getting out.

Shawnee glanced to the east. The dust cloud was closing steadily. Then he looked south to see Cletus riding hard alongside the chuck wagon, but Sil and the remuda were nowhere in sight. When Shawnee again turned east, he could make out the shapes of the riders raising the dust. It was them.

As Cletus and the chuck wagon reached the canyon entrance, Shawnee pulled the Henry from its scabbard and shouted to be heard. "That's them, Get ready for a fight."

Cletus ordered the cook to move the chuck wagon in front of the entrance and told the hands to take up firing spots under and around it. Shawnee joined them, crouching next to Cletus.

The Indians began a hooping, loud enough to be heard over the noise of their horses as they charged full on. Gunfire erupted from both sides. Bullets whizzed and hit close to the crew. Arrows imbedded themselves into the wood wagon and the ground in front of it. On the first pass, several Indians, fighting in the open, fell wounded or dead. None of the cowboys sustained injury.

Cletus let his attention stray to his concern for Sil who had still not arrived with the remuda. As he tried to spot him, an arrow came close enough for the fletching to brush his head. He flinched back.

Shawnee, at Cletus's side, saw another attacker setting up for a riding shot, aiming a long gun at Cletus. Shawnee's rifle bullet took the assailant off his horse. Cletus ducked back down behind the wagon. "Thanks."

The attackers rode past to the north as the remuda came closer. Several of them, sighting the remuda, turned to head for that prize.

Shawnee and Cletus both saw the move at the same time. Concerned for Sil, they mounted and darted out away from the wagon. Firing their pistols rapidly, they tried to drive the Indians away before they reached the remuda. This finally worked. Shawnee and Cletus rode flat out for the remuda, now in plain sight. Sil was nowhere to be seen.

The remuda horses scattered in all directions. As Shawnee and Cletus rode through the dust, Sil came into their view. He lay spread eagle on the ground, several arrows impaling his upper body. They hauled rein and dropped out of the saddle, trotting toward Sil's side.

"No, no, no!" Cletus shouted as they ran.

As they reached Sil, they could see, in addition to the arrows, he had taken several bullet wounds. They crouched beside him. A sick feeling came into the pit of Shawnee's stomach.

Sil was barely there. Pale and obviously hurting, he opened his eyes to peer up at them. "Hey, *amigos,*"His voice was faint, breathless. "Hell of a fight.... I don't... do so good."

"Shut up, Sil," Cletus said sharply. "Don't talk. We'll—"

Sil's head fell to the side, his eyes still open. Shawnee checked for a pulse but found none. He looked at Cletus and shook his head, then reached down to close Sil's eyes.

Cletus growled something sounding like, "Shit!"

"I shoulda came back to him sooner." Shawnee glanced around at several Indian bodies on the ground nearby. "Reckon he got his licks in anyhow."

Cletus ground his teeth. "No, he didn't. And it ain't your fault. I'm the one put him back here. He's... gone 'cause of me."

"You can't do that, Cletus. It could a been any one of us." As he spoke, a sound caught Shawnee's attention. He glanced over his shoulder to see a lone Indian riding at them, a pistol in his hand. Quickly, Shawnee surmised the man's purpose. In one motion, he shoved Cletus aside and pulled his Colt as a ball cut into the dirt in the exact spot where Cletus had crouched. Shawnee's gun came up. He fired point blank at the Indian. The man's body pitched to the side, off his horse. As it hit the ground, Shawnee placed another shot into it.

Cletus rolled to his knees and looked around. There was amazement on his face. "Twiced in one day. I surely owes you."

"Nah." Shawnee shrugged.

More rapid gunfire in the distance drew their attention. They scrambled to their feet and remounted, setting out for the herd. Halfway there, the firing stopped. They galloped into the area to see the crew out from cover, crowded together.

As Shawnee and Cletus rode up, a stranger emerged from the middle of the group of cowboys. He appeared to be an Indian from his coloring, but his clothes were a combination of native garb and military uniform. The blue tunic appeared to be that of a Union soldier and bore the three yellow stripes of a sergeant's rank sewn on the sleeves.

Cletus approached the man. "Who're you?"

"Sergeant Joe Two-Trees, Indian Police. We work for the Indian Agency. They sent us tracking them renegades a week back. Guess we got here just in time. You running this outfit?"

Cletus nodded. "Cletus Workman, trail boss. We're out of Texas, trailing this herd to market in Kansas."

"Well, you won't have no more trouble from them renegades. My men'll nail 'em for sure. Thanks for holding them while we catched up."

"Wasn't what we was aiming for, but I reckon it worked out that-a-way."

"Look, I got to get on to my troop. Good luck to you." The policeman started toward his horse. He mounted and rode off in the direction taken by his men in pursuit of the marauders. The dust rising from the chase in progress could be seen in the distance.

14

AFTER PRESSING THE COOK INTO service to care for several scrapes and minor bullet wounds sustained by the drovers, Cletus led a small party, carrying shovels, back to where Sil had fallen. They dug a shallow grave nearby and placed Sil's body gently in it for his last rest. Shawnee stayed back with the rest of the crew until Cletus sent for them to assemble for the funeral. Those who participated in the grave digging were closer to Sil than Shawnee was. He elected to allow them privacy in their last act in Sil's behalf.

As they gathered around the freshly covered grave and removed their hats, Cletus placed some stones at the head as a marker. Standing behind the stones, Cletus opened the bible he had earlier pulled from his saddlebag to the spot marked by the ribbon. Holding it open, he spoke to the crew.

"You all knowed Sil, but I reckon I knowed him longer, better. He never had a bad word for nobody, not man nor horse. He done his job the best he knowed how, and he was always there when he was needed. He died doing what he loved doing best, taking care of horses. He's with you now, Lord, and no doubt better off, but we'll surely miss him."

Cletus cleared his throat and read the twenty-third Psalm. The group bowed their heads. Some stood perfectly still, some shuffled uncomfortably, but all displayed respect for their comrade and sorrow for his passing. When the service concluded, each man wandered off in his own direction to reflect on the loss of a friend. After a few minutes, Cletus assigned a few men to round up the scattered remuda horses. Then he asked for volunteers, needing one man to run the remuda. He got several and picked one, a young cowboy who liked Sil and wanted to complete Sil's job.

Shawnee joined Gray, standing nearby. "Well, Gray, we ain't going to be seeing Sil no more. I know you thought a lot of him. I did too, but we got to move along without him." It seemed Gray understood Shawnee's words, nodding and nickering.

The crew regrouped at the chuck wagon and prepared to get the herd under way. Shawnee rode north for further scouting while Cletus gave the order to move out.

Throughout the rest of the drive, there were no further violent incidents. There were, however, occurrences normally encountered on cattle drives. Toward the end of the Indian Territory, they rode through a major rainstorm, experiencing difficulty keeping the herd from stampeding due to frightening thunder and lightning. At its worst, the storm forced Cletus to halt the drive until the weather broke, losing two days travel time.

Through trial and error, Shawnee led the drive into Kansas. Once they were there, he stayed closer to the herd because he knew the general lay of this land from his earlier trip to Texas. The crew kept up a steady push northward.

An incident in central Kansas presented the possibility of a delay. A farmer refused to allow the herd to cross his land, concerned the cattle would trample all his crops. Cletus agreed to skirt the beeves around the fields in question, pressing Shawnee into service to find a route around the farm. Shawnee did so but was unable to lead the drive completely off the farmer's land without taking it days out of the way. The farmer allowed the use of his land as long as it skirted around his plantings. He demanded a fee for the crossing. Cletus paid the man from the funds Tell had advanced at the start of the drive.

Finally reaching the vicinity of Abilene on the tenth of August, Cletus halted the cattle in the middle of the Kansas plains, several miles south of the town. He joined Shawnee at the front of the herd, elated.

"I don't know how we done it, but we five days ahead of schedule."

"Well, that's good, ain't it?"

"I ain't even sure they ready for us in Abilene. Got to find out from the buyer." Cletus reached into his pocket for the contract. "Fellow name a Gilliam, Desmond Gilliam. Says here he'll be at the hotel."

"Might be good you go see this Mister Gilliam."

"Yeah, might be good you do that."

Shawnee looked at his boss with uncertainty. "You use the right word there? Sounded like you said you, meaning me."

"You heerd me right."

"That ain't right. You're the foreman. You're the—"

"Yeah, the nigga foreman, that's me. That's what he'll see, a black man. How far you think I'll get with that kind a baggage?"

"Come on, Cletus, war's over. Ain't no more slaves."

"Right, war's over, but the feelings ain't. Folks still looks down on a black man, and they sure as hell ain't going to make no cattle deal with one."

Shawnee now understood what Cletus was proposing. "So, you want me to go in your place?"

"Yeah."

Shawnee was quiet for a few moments, considering the exposure a mission like this would cause him. Besides being a wanted man, he had no idea how to conduct himself in a deal like this. If he was discovered, an entire town would be on him, and he would never be able to settle with Teverence. He had to get out of this.

"No, Cletus. I didn't sign on for that."

Cletus leaned forward in the saddle. "You signed on to deliver this herd to Abilene, whatever it takes. What it's going to take is you go ahead on to Abilene and deal with Mister Gilliam, 'cause if I goes, he'll throw me the hell out for a fact. It's got to be you, ain't no other choice."

"Cletus, you said you owe me—"

"True enough, but Mister Tell's counting on us, all of us, to pull this off, and that's more important. Now, I'm the trail boss here, Shawnee. I say what goes, and I'm telling you, you *will* do this."

"Cletus—"

"Or you'll deal with me and wind up doing it anyhow. You savvy?"

Boxed in between his desire for revenge and his sense of duty, Shawnee knew the only way out of this was to tell Cletus his entire history, the reason for his reluctance, but he was not prepared to do that at this point. "I savvy. I just ain't responsible for what might happen."

Cletus leaned back in the saddle. He handed the contract over to Shawnee. "Whatever happen, leastwise, I knows you done your best. Now, get on outta here."

Reluctantly, Shawnee took the paper and put Gray in motion.

Abilene in 1865 was just another Kansas plains farm town. It contained a few ramshackle buildings, either businesses depending on the surrounding farms for their existence or the residences of those business owners. It boasted no conveniences, such as a decent restaurant, and very few commercial structures, most notably a small local bank, a couple of slop eateries, and a single hotel. The Abilene House was nothing more than a two story wood affair offering sparsely furnished, seldom cleaned rooms. The local cockroaches claimed credit as the most frequent boarders of the establishment.

Shawnee entered the only street of the town and rode slowly. There was nothing remarkable about this place, like so many other towns he had passed through on his way across Kansas to Texas. In fact, it reminded him of Shawneetown before the first Quantrill raid. Concerned with the possibility of being recognized or identified, he started searching for the hotel.

The sign outside the building was more than large enough to be seen plainly. The thought that a blind man couldn't miss it occurred to Shawnee. He stopped Gray at the short hitch rail and dismounted, noting there were no other horses tied there. As a precaution, he glanced around for anything out of the ordinary, a practice he had long since utilized before proceeding wherever he went. He saw nothing, so he entered.

The interior of the building was no different from the outside, except for being less weather beaten. The walls were unpainted. There were a few straight-backed wood chairs placed around, only one of which was occupied. A staircase on the side led to the second floor landing on which doors to the rooms could be seen. Directly to the rear, a long, waist-high table served as the clerk's desk. An overweight, bald man stood behind it.

The man occupying the chair was dressed better than was the norm for this location. His hair was gray, his face long and bony. Tall and lanky, he wore a dark suit and a brocade cravat with a diamond stickpin to hold it in place. He held his homburg hat on his lap, somewhat primly.

Shawnee stopped upon entering to survey the room. The man in the chair had to be Gilliam. Shawnee went directly to him. He looked up as Shawnee approached.

"How do. Are you,"—Shawnee opened the contract to refresh his memory—"Desmond Gilliam?"

"Who wants to know?" The man had a deep, sneering voice.

Not about to give his real name or his alias, Shawnee thought fast. "Cletus Workman, trail boss for the Tell herd a couple miles south of town."

Gilliam smiled. "Yes, I'm Gilliam. You're early."

"Yes, sir, by five days, I reckon. Just letting you know we here."

Gilliam rose and shook Shawnee's gloved hand. "That's good, real good as a matter of fact. That'll give me even more of a jump on McCoy."

Shawnee was not sure what exact;y the man's meaning was. "Come again?"

"McCoy. Joe McCoy," Gilliam sounded almost as if Shawnee should know the name. "Thinks he's got the beef market all sewn up. He's trying to get the Kansas Pacific to build a spur line into Abilene so he can ship cattle to Chicago direct from here." Gilliam's face showed anger and determination. "Well, maybe he's got more capital than I have, but I moved faster. I'll be first to Chicago, and I'll set the market."

Shawnee failed to comprehend the statement. "Don't know nothing 'bout setting no market, Mister Gilliam. I'm just here letting you know we waiting on you to inspect the herd and pay for 'em. Then you're welcome to take the beeves over, and we'll be on our way."

Gilliam took in a breath to compose himself. "Yes, of course. When can I see the herd?"

Shawnee shrugged. "Your call."

Gilliam cracked a slight smile. "I'll get a horse from the livery stable and meet you back here. We'll go now."

They walked to the door and stepped outside. As Gilliam walked away, Shawnee shook his head once, trying to understand the man's motives. Within minutes, Gilliam returned. Shawnee regarded the man dressed in the suit, mounted on the rented horse. Sure looked funny up there, but the expression on his face defied anyone to tell him that. Shawnee stepped up on Gray, and they rode up the street.

On the way out of town, Shawnee glanced at signs which identified some of the buildings. One sign caught his eye, Abilene Hardware. The name of the proprietor was familiar to him, Otto Daylock. With a name that unusual, it had to be the same Otto Daylock that beat the stuffing out of him the day they hung his father. It warranted him coming back to pay a call on Mr. Daylock.

The ride to the herd's location was slow. Gilliam was not a proficient rider. He needed to stop to rest twice during the short journey. When they arrived, Gilliam asked the aid of a few drovers to move the cattle past him for a count. Shawnee allowed it while he joined Cletus near the chuckwagon.

"How'd it go?"

"All right, I reckon. I don't know half of what he's talking 'bout."

"Don't matter. Long as he pays for the beef, I don't care what he's got to say."

Gilliam returned from the herd an hour later. "I'm satisfied. I count three thousand and fourteen head, all in good shape." He reached into his jacket and came out with an envelope. "This contains my check for the computed amount." He handed it to Shawnee.

Shawnee took it and, trying to appear as if he knew what he was doing, opened it, and read the check. The amount appeared to have been freshly entered. Seventy-five thousand three hundred and fifty dollars! Shit! He didn't think so much money existed. To make certain the amount was correct, he re-examined the contract which gave the price per head. Verification in his head took a couple of attempts, but he managed to figure it.

"Is there a problem?" Gilliam seemed anxious.

"No, sir. I just don't cipher so quick as some. It figures out fine."

"Good. I'll have to ask you to stay with the herd one more day. I have a crew arriving to drive the cattle to the nearest railhead, but they won't get here until tomorrow. I wasn't expecting you to be early. Can you stay on?"

Shawnee glanced at Cletus and quickly picked up the black man's slight nod. Shawnee turned back to Gilliam. "I reckon so."

Gilliam shook hands with Shawnee and turned his horse toward Abilene. As soon as the dealer was out of sight, Shawnee handed the check over to Cletus. "Here, take this. Don't want it burning no hole in my hand."

Cletus chuckled. "You done real good, Shawnee. Now, all we gots to do is wait till his crew shows up, and we can head on home to Texas."

"I need to use that time, Cletus. I got something to tend to in Abilene, personal-like." He hoped Cletus didn't get curious about what he'd be doing in Abilene and start asking questions he wasn't ready to answer.

"Reckon it'll be all right. Just see you're back here 'fore dark tomorrow so's you can get paid with the rest of the crew."

Shawnee smiled. "Sure thing. Don't want to miss that." He turned Gray toward Abilene and started out at a trot, uncertain how this encounter would play out.

A short time later, Shawnee pulled Gray up at the hitch rail outside Daylock's store and dismounted. As he tied the horse off, he glanced around to again be sure no one was observing him. He went in and immediately stepped to the side of the door to scan the room, trying to get the lay of it.

It was disorder, with hardware items of every size and category crammed together on the selling floor. Just like the one in Shawnee. Along the walls, at least in some orderly fashion, tools were hung on display. In the rear, behind a makeshift wood counter, Otto Daylock stood conducting business with a customer.

Daylock glanced over as Shawnee entered but showed no sign of recognition. He was the same as Shawnee remembered him, maybe a little pudgier, stooped a bit more, but the features were unchanged.

Shawnee pretended to browse in order to blend in with his surroundings, waiting for the customer to leave. His business with Daylock would be conducted in private.

"Thanks, Otto." The customer picked up his package. "Be seeing you."

"You bet." Daylock's deep, smoky voice seemed to fit his size.

The customer walked to the door and let himself out. Quickly, Shawnee moved to the door and engaged the lock.

"How can I help you, young fellow?" Daylock moved around from the counter.

Shawnee turned to face the man. "Been a long time, Daylock."

Daylock stopped halfway to Shawnee. "How's that?"

Shawnee closed the distance. "You don't remember me, huh?"

Daylock squinted. "You do look a tad familiar, but—"

"Three years back up in Shawneetown. You beat the shit out of me just before you and the rest of them Jayhawkers hung my pa."

Shawnee watched as his words triggered Daylock's memory and caused his inquisitive expression to change to concern.

"Pearce." Daylock lowered his voice almost to a whisper.

"Right." Shawnee nodded. "Lon Pearce."

Shawnee took a step forward. Daylock backed up, suddenly seeming smaller to Shawnee.

"What do you want?" Daylock had a quiver of fear in his voice.

"Time to settle up, Daylock." Shawnee took another step closer.

"Look, you got to understand. It was war. We was only doing what we had to do."

"Sure you was. And you didn't enjoy it one bit, did you?"

"I—"

"Bullshit! You couldn't wait to hang my pa. Didn't even give him a trial or nothing. And you had a real good time beating up on his kid, didn't you? Well, like I said, time to settle up."

Daylock shrank back. "What're you going to do?"

Shawnee moved closer, now within grabbing distance. "That'll be up to you."

"I ain't armed."

"You don't see me going for a gun, do you?"

Daylock did not reply.

"You beat me senseless once. Now it's my turn."

Daylock took a breath, appearing to weigh his odds in a fist fight. Then, suddenly, he swung a wide right at Shawnee's face. Shawnee, putting Cletus's lessons to practice, blocked the punch and immediately shot a short right jab to Daylock's nose. The blow snapped Daylock's head back. Shawnee shot another straight shot to the man's chin. Daylock bounded back a few feet.

Now Shawnee had the measure of the man, slow, uncoordinated. He followed Daylock, delivering two left jabs and a right cross to Daylock's head. Daylock spun around and careened into the counter, landing on his elbows, his back to Shawnee.

As Shawnee closed on him, Daylock grabbed a hammer resting on the counter. He turned quickly and heaved the object at Shawnee. Sidestepping it, Shawnee kept going, ducking low and pushing a solid left into Daylock's stomach as the hammer clattered on the floor behind him.

The blow doubled Daylock and sapped his breath. Shawnee straightened up, bringing a right uppercut with him, catching the older man under the chin and lifting him up and over the counter.

The big man dropped heavily on the floor, leaving the counter between them.

Shawnee, winded from the activity, sucked in air and propped
his hands on his knees to recover. As he heard noises from behind
the counter and looked up, Daylock rose, clumsily fumbling with a
small handgun, trying to cock it. Shawnee reacted, pulling his Colt
from its holster. Daylock got his weapon primed and fired a wild shot
in Shawnee's direction. Shawnee leveled his gun and fired. Daylock
yelped and fell back against the shelves, dislodging small items that
clattered on the floor around him. As Shawnee watched, Daylock
dropped his pistol and slowly sank to the floor.

15

S HAWNEE'S EARS RANG FROM THE sound of the two shots in close quarters as Daylock dropped to the floor. Locked in place for a moment, Shawnee recovered and vaulted over the counter to examine Daylock.

He never had any intention of killing the man, only using his fists to repay Daylock for the beating Daylock had dealt him three years earlier. Now he had shot Daylock, causing himself two more problems. The sound of the shots put him in danger of discovery before he could slip away, and, if Daylock died, there would be no answer to the question Shawnee had to ask him.

He crouched beside Daylock and checked the wound his shot had inflicted. Blood oozed from the hole in Daylock's lower left side. It was serious but likely not a killing wound. Good.

Daylock's eyes locked on Shawnee's. "Don't kill me. Please."

"I ain't going to kill you. I'll get you help, but I want an answer first."

Daylock appeared to be confused and dazed. "To what?"

"Carl Teverence. Where is he?"

"Teverence?"

"Yeah, Teverence. The leader of the Jayhawkers that hung my pa and killed my ma. That Teverence. Where he be?"

Daylock hesitated.

Shawnee lost patience. He grabbed Daylock's shirt and lifted him slightly, causing the man pain as the wound was stretched and shifted. Daylock grimaced. Shawnee gritted his teeth. "Where?"

Daylock raised his hand, silently requesting Shawnee to let go. Shawnee lowered him to the floor.

"I ain't seen him since I left Shawnee a year ago. He was still there then. Still had his feed and grain place."

"No lies."

"I ain't lying. Far as I know, he's still in Shawnee. But I ain't seen him recent. Honest to God."

Shawnee released Daylock's shirt and got up. "Don't go nowheres." He spun on his butt over the counter and headed for the door. In one quick move, he unlocked and opened the door. As he went to Gray, he glanced around and spotted a man walking toward him.

"Hey, there," he called as he mounted. "They's a wounded man inside there. Needs help."

The passerby heard him and reacted, hurrying to the entrance of the store.

Shawnee pulled Gray around and set out up the street at a gallop. He kept up the pace over the few miles from Abilene to the site of the Tell drive camp. As he rode in, Cletus stepped away from the chuckwagon toward him. Shawnee pulled Gray up hard and dropped from the saddle.

"'Pears like you got half of Abilene on your tail."

"I might just." Shawnee was breathless.

"What's that supposed to mean?"

"Means I got to disappear, pronto."

"You're talking in riddles. Settle down and make sense, will you?"

Shawnee took a deep breath and made a decision. "All right, look,

I got a heap to tell you and a short time to do it in, so listen up. Three years ago...."

In the next ten minutes, Shawnee told Cletus everything about himself, from the hanging of his father to his run-in with Daylock less than an hour earlier. Cletus silently took in the information.

Shawnee finished his story by saying, "I only come back here 'cause I figured I owed you some kind a explaining. You been a good friend to me, Cletus. Didn't want to leave you high and dry, not knowing nothing."

Cletus scratched his head. "It's good you told me, but I don't reckon you're any much different than most of the waddies in this outfit. I'm sure they all got stories like yours they can tell if they're a mind to. Look, we'll be out of these parts and heading back to Texas tomorrow. You lay low till then and come on back with us. You'll be safe there."

"Can't do that. I made Mister Tell a promise. If my past came back on me, I won't involve him or his. I got a thing to do, and I got to go it alone."

"No, you don't. Shit. Mister Tell don't know nothing 'bout this, and he ain't going to, not from me, leastwise. You come on back to the ranch. Ain't nobody'll touch you there. 'Sides, I knows Chrissie be right glad to see you."

"There's the other reason I can't go back. I can't saddle her with my woes. What I got to do ain't in Texas."

Cletus let out a breath as he stopped to think. "Then take what's owed you and whatever provisions you can tote. You'll need 'em sure. I owes you at least that much for twiced saving my hide. Anybody comes out here asking after you, we ain't seed you."

"All right. Thanks."

Cletus instructed the cook to pack provisions to be secured to Gray's saddle while he counted out Shawnee's pay for the drive. It amounted to over five hundred dollars. Shawnee allowed as how it would keep him independent for long enough to get to where he was heading.

"Just curious. Where you heading?"

"Likely Shawneetown," Shawnee replied as he mounted. "Wherever I can find Carl Teverence."

Cletus reached his hand up to shake Shawnee's hand, grasping it tightly. "You watch your back."

"I will. *Adios.*"

"Y usted, amigo."

Shawnee urged Gray forward, heading northeast. He looked back over his shoulder to see the camp and his friend slowly blend into the Kansas horizon.

FOR NEARLY TWO WEEKS, SHAWNEE rode steadily without stopping in any of the towns he passed. He depended on the supplies provided by the Tell outfit and his ability to supplement by hunting small animals. Then some of the staples, coffee and flour, as well as powder and ball ran low. He was forced to stop to replenish, choosing a small settlement called Ford's Wells.

Planning to secure the needed items and get clear of the town quickly, he went directly to the general store. He dismounted and tied Gray to the hitch rail while glancing around to check for unwanted eyes, then stepped to the open door of the establishment.

To his right, on the wall adjacent to the door, he caught sight of something. It stopped him dead in his tracks. Affixed to the wall at eye level was a wanted poster. *Wanted! For attempted murder. Alonso Pearce.* In the center of the page, just above his name was a drawing of his likeness leaving little to the imagination. Couldn't be plainer if it was a tintype. Shit! They surely circulated them quick-like.

His immediate reaction, which he initially followed, was to get the hell out of there, but, when he reached Gray, he stopped and questioned the move. Should he sneak away before being recognized or should he take the chance most ordinary people never pay attention to wanted posters, thereby securing the supplies he needed? The decision consumed only seconds. He went back to the store entrance and stepped inside.

Several customers were involved in making purchases. None paid him notice. He walked to the counter in the back.

The bearded man behind it addressed him, "How do, stranger. What can I do you for?"

"Need a couple pounds of coffee, couple pounds of flour, and a pound of salt and a box of forty-four Henry rounds and powder and ball for a thirty-six Navy."

The bearded man looked straight at Shawnee, appearing to commit the list to memory. "Sure thing," He went to work on the order.

Trying not to seem nervous or to stand out, Shawnee wandered to the side of the store and browsed over some leather items hanging on the wall.

Within minutes, the store clerk had assembled the food items. "Will there be anything else?" He brought the ammunition to the counter.

Shawnee returned to the counter. "That's the all of it. How much?"

The clerk ciphered quickly. "Four dollars and thirty cents."

Shawnee counted out the cash and handed it over. He wrapped his arms around the items and pulled them into his chest and then turned and walked outside. Behind him, the clerk called to a customer. "Hey, Sam, come here a minute."

Shawnee balanced the supplies and moved to Gray. Finding it almost impossible to store them away in his saddlebags without first setting them down, he squatted and placed them on the ground. One by one, he lifted and placed them into the pouches, losing more time than he had anticipated. The saddlebags were strained and bulging as he tightened the last bag strap and loosed Gray's reins. He was about to put his foot in the stirrup when an unfamiliar voice spoke behind him.

"Hold up a minute there, young fellow." It was a soft, pleasant voice but with a commanding tone.

Shawnee froze in place. Then he turned to face the voice. A tall, somewhat overweight man in dark dress clothes and a collarless white shirt stood about four feet away. He had a round, boyish face showing several days growth of beard. Under his bowler hat strands of blond hair stuck out in all directions. On his left lapel, a silver colored badge with the word "Marshal" on it stood out against the dark cloth background.

"Let's have a look at you," the marshal said.

Shawnee stood still and said nothing.

The marshal had his hand on the butt of the gun in his hip holster. He pulled out a folded sheet of paper and flipped it open. Shawnee guessed it was the same poster he had just seen on the wall minutes earlier. Shit! Bad call. The lawman was silent for a moment, gazing over the poster. The quick squawk of leather reached Shawnee's ears as the marshal lifted the revolver from the holster and leveled it on Shawnee.

"Thought so. You're Alonso Pearce, wanted for attempted murder in Abilene. Damn good likeness, I'd say. Now, don't you move a muscle. You're under arrest."

"You got it wrong, Marshal. I didn't do what that paper says. I—"

"I'm not judge nor jury, Pearce. I'm arresting you and holding you for the Abilene authorities. You'll be tried all legal and proper. You'll have your say then. Right now, like I said, don't move a muscle. That includes your jaw."

As he spoke, the marshal stepped in and reached out to take Shawnee's sidearm. With the marshal's gun aimed straight at his belly, Shawnee saw no move available to him that would not get him gutshot. He stood his ground as the revolver left his holster. The marshal stepped back.

"Here's how this is going to work. The jail's up the street." He gestured with his gun to indicate the direction behind him. "You're going to walk there with your hands in the air. I'll be right behind you. Try something, anything, and I'll put one in your leg. That'll stop you. Now, get to moving."

The longer Shawnee let this carry on, the less possible his chance for escape became. He had to do something to turn the tables on the lawman. It had to be something unexpected, something to take the man by surprise. He thought hard, and fast.

"Gray, *arriba!*'

At Shawnee's order, Gray reared, front hooves flailing. The close proximity of the horse to the marshal caused the man to instinctively step back. He tripped over his own foot and stumbled backward, landing on his butt, losing his hold on both pistols as his hands went back to break the fall. Shawnee moved quickly as Gray settled down. He stooped and grabbed both guns and then stood over the lawman with both weapons trained on him.

The marshal propped himself on one elbow. Fear lodged in his eyes, but he did not cower. "You going to kill me, kid?"

The words burned into Shawnee's mind. Did he think about killing this man? Yeah, for a second, but, shit, he was only doing what they paid him for. He had no axe to grind, even said as much. Couldn't fault a man for doing his job, doing it fair-like. Still, he would not get very far if the marshal was able to give an alarm for help. He'd be stopped before he made it up the street.

Holstering his gun, Shawnee leaned in and swung a short hard right fist into the marshal's face, smacking him on the jaw, opening a cut at the corner of his mouth. It tore the man's head to the side and dumped him on his back. He appeared stunned, maybe unconscious.

"Sorry, Marshal." Shawnee dropped the lawman's gun on the ground. He picked up Gray's reins and swung up into the saddle. Immediately, Gray went into a gallop, taking Shawnee up the street and out of Ford's Wells.

Damn it! That there just done it. No coming back from it. Full blown outlaw now if he wasn't before. Only one thing mattered now, he had to bring Teverence down any way he could before the law did the same to him.

16

SHAWNEE MADE NO FURTHER STOPS. Pointing Gray directly northeast, he rode constantly from dawn to sundown each day, stopping only to care for Gray, to eat and drink, and to hunt and trap small game for fresh meat. He lost track of the number of days he had been on the trail. Nothing mattered except reaching his destination without encountering the law.

He came into familiar surroundings. This route would take him straight across the land owned by Toby Joe Hawks.

It had been three years since he'd left and headed for Texas, three years since he'd seen Toby Joe. It was only a few days he'd spent with him, learning about guns. But those days and Toby Joe's teachings had shaped his thinking and his reasoning. Because of Toby Joe, he'd been able to stay alive. He wondered if the old man was still there.

It was mid-morning when Shawnee came up on the Hawks spread. He had to make the time to see Toby Joe again, to assure himself the old timer was well and not in any difficulty. Continuing across the property, he approached Hawks's cabin. It was rundown, untended, several of the roof shingles were missing. As he rode in, no hides hung on the drying racks, and, indeed, the racks themselves had rot and missing slats in several spots. If Toby Joe still resided here, this was not looking good.

Shawnee stopped Gray near the cabin and got down. He dropped the reins and gave the horse a hand signal to stand in place, then he walked to the cabin door. He was uncertain what he would find inside, but it likely wouldn't be good. He hesitated before knocking.

"Who's that?" The voice was definitely Toby Joe's, but it sounded weary, even weak.

"Toby Joe, it's… Lon, Lon Pearce."

"Lon Pearce? Well, what you standing out there for? Come on in."

Shawnee stepped inside, preoccupied with the fact he had just used his given name for the first time in years.

Hawks sat at the small table which was in the same position as the last time Shawnee had been here. A swath of leather stretched across the table in front of him. His embossing tools lay idle off to the side.

Shawnee gazed at the man. He looked much older than three years ought to make him. His face was contorted in pain. There was a significant growth of beard, and his clothes were torn and soiled.

"Toby Joe, what's wrong?" Shawnee made no attempt to hide the concern in his voice.

"Ain't doing so good, Lon. Damn leg's done caught up with me."

Shawnee moved closer. Hawks's stiff leg, with a bare foot, protruded from under the table. The foot was red and swollen. A makeshift crutch was propped against the table.

"Can't get around so good no more."

"How long's it been like that?"

"A good while, I reckon. Couple of weeks now I ain't been able to do more'n hobble around."

"You seen a doc about it?"

"Can't afford no doc, Lon. Ain't been hunting in a month. This here's the last hide I got. Got to finish this job so's I can get paid and lay in some supplies. Ain't sure what I'll do after."

"Looks like I come back just in time."

"How's that?"

"I surely know how to hunt, and I got money for supplies and a doc. We'll get you through this."

Hawks leaned back in the chair, a smile displacing the pain on his face.

"Well, fancy you now, all growed up and decked out like a cowhand. I'd bet you're a good 'un, too. What brings you back here anyhow?"

"Teverence. I'm ready to take him."

"Shit! I was hoping sending you to Texas'd clear him out a your head."

"Toby Joe, he never left my head these three years, but he can wait a mite now. You're more important."

"Don't waste no time on me, Lon. You ought to be getting shed of here—"

"No! I'm here, and I'm helping, and I don't want to hear no arguing."

"Hooeee! You surely done growed up, I'll say that. Ain't no way I want to get on your bad side. You done growed a pair."

Shawnee fed and stabled Gray. He brought his saddlebags into the cabin and unloaded the supplies he had left. As he placed them on the shelf on the side of the room where Hawks kept his foodstuffs, he mingled them with the meager number already there. Using Hawks's equipment, he mixed up a batch of batter and cooked pancakes and bacon. He refused Hawks's offer of assistance.

"Cowboying ain't the only thing I done learned in Texas."

Hawks ate his fill. Clearly his diet had suffered due to his inability to move about.

"I'll go hunting after we're done eating. 'Sides food, what do you need to keep working?"

"Elk hide, I reckon." Hawks pointed to the hide clumped on the floor beside him. "Yonder's elk."

"I'll see what I can round up."

Hawks swallowed his last bite and smiled. "Glad you're back, Lon, but I sort of wisht you wasn't."

"How's that?"

"Well, what you said about Teverence, I got to tell you, he'll be a lot harder to get to now. He owns most of Shawneetown, half the county as well. Got a bunch of gunsels on his payroll, and the sheriff's in his pocket."

"Toby Joe, I been down a heap of trails since I left here. I'll figure it out."

Hawks nodded. "Yup, you just might at that."

—————————

OVER THE NEXT WEEK, SHAWNEE spent most of his time hunting, bringing down an elk and a mule deer. Under Hawks's instructions, Shawnee skinned the carcasses and racked the hides to dry and cure. He smoked and stored the meat, enough for several weeks.

It was morning when Hawks finished the leather job he had been working on.

They rolled the leather up. Shawnee moved a chair out onto the porch and then helped Hawks out to it to sit in the sun.

"I'll deliver it for you."

"I'm obliged to you. It's the Ross farm, due west of here about a three-hour ride."

Shawnee tied a rawhide thong around the piece.

"I should be back by suppertime. How much he owe you?"

"Fifty."

Shawnee lifted the piece and started for the stable. "See you tonight." He mounted Gray and rode out.

He followed Hawks's directions and watched the trail signs to locate the customer. After making the delivery and collecting the amount due, he started back to Hawks's place.

Approaching from the west gave him a clear view of the front of the cabin from quite a distance away, even at dusk. Two men on horses sat in front of Hawks who was still on the porch. One had a tan colored suit and a narrow brimmed hat. His shape looked familiar to Shawnee. The other one wore dark clothes and a bowler hat.

Curious, Shawnee halted Gray and dismounted, dropping the reins so the horse would stay in place. Pulling the Henry from its saddle holster and moving carefully on foot, Shawnee advanced quickly to a hiding position behind the stable. It was the same place he'd hidden in three years earlier. He crouched and listened.

"You know you ain't welcome here." Hawks spoke to one of the riders. "Never was, truth be told."

"I'm willing to put our differences aside, Hawks," the man in tan said.

The voice was familiar to Shawnee, very familiar. Teverence! He was right there. He could have taken him down right now, but, no, he wanted him to know where it came from, who was doing it and why. And he didn't want Toby Joe in the middle of it.

Teverence continued. "I'm here to make you an offer. Sheriff tells me you owe about three hundred in back taxes. I'll cancel the tax bill and give you five hundred cash. Just sign the deed over right here, right now. That'll give you a two hundred dollar profit. What do you say?"

Hawks's look was intense. "I say no. Definite no. Now you take your god damn gunslinger there and you get your asses off my land. Now."

"You ain't in no position to be belligerent, Hawks. Now, I'm making you the offer one more time…."

Shawnee raised the rifle to his shoulder and sighted on Teverence's back. He levered a round into the chamber, loud enough to be heard.

Teverence's body tightened as he seemed to recognize the sound.

"He said no." Shawnee's voice was loud, ominous. "Now, get moving out of here."

Teverence moved slightly to call over his shoulder.

"You're butting in things don't concern you, stranger. I'd advise you to back off and let this be."

"Case you ain't ciphered things yet, they's a rifle aimed dead at your back, Teverence. Get the hell out of here and take your friend with you, or I'll drop you both right there."

Teverence hesitated.

"Make up your mind. I ain't waiting."

Teverence motioned to his companion and said something inaudible to him. They pulled their horses around and started riding away.

"Hawks, this ain't over." Teverence shook his fist at Hawks.

Shawnee watched carefully from his hiding spot as they moved. When they left his field of vision, he quickly went to the other side of the stable. From there, he was able to view them as they picked up speed and rode off toward the northeast. He waited until they were completely gone, then he stepped out from cover and lowered the hammer of the rifle as he hurried toward Hawks.

Glancing over his shoulder, he let out a short whistle and called out, "Gray, come on, boy."

Hawks sat with a big grin on his face. "You surely cowed him."

Shawnee was more concerned with this new development. "You should have told me about the taxes."

Hawks seemed more interested in Teverence's reaction. "He knowed it was you." He chuckled. "I seen it in his face."

"Toby Joe, without you payin' them taxes, he can send the sheriff out here and take your place legal."

"He can try."

As Hawks spoke, Gray reached Shawnee. Shawnee rubbed the horse's forehead and then replaced the rifle in its scabbard. "He'll do more'n try. We'll need to be ready."

After breakfast the next morning, Shawnee placed Hawks in the chair in the cabin doorway with a loaded twelve gauge coach gun across his lap. "Keep an eye peeled while I take care of the stock. Anybody shows up, holler and hit the floor. I'll take care of the rest."

"Ain't no way you're handling this alone."

"You ain't in no shape for a fight. Stay clear of it and trust you learned me right. I know what I'm doing."

Hawks nodded.

Shawnee went to the stable and fed the animals. It was quiet for about ten minutes. As Shawnee brushed Gray down, Hawks called out, "Riders coming."

Shawnee turned toward the horizon. A group of six horsemen came fast. Too close. Why did Toby Joe wait so long to sing out? He glanced toward Hawks, still in the chair. "Toby Joe, get down."

Hawks did not move from the chair. He raised the shotgun. "Lon, this is my fight. I ain't backing down."

Shawnee pulled the Henry from his nearby saddle and ducked behind a rain barrel. By now, the group was only a few yards away. The rider in the lead had a badge. It reflected the sun like a mirror. Likely he was the sheriff. Shawnee hoped this didn't go sideways.

The sheriff halted the group far enough back so any talking would need to be shouted. "Hawks, I see you there." His voice was gruff and scratchy. "No need for guns. I come to talk."

"This is my property, Sheriff," Hawks said. "I'll keep the gun. State your business from where you're at."

The sheriff shifted nervously in his saddle. "I got two things to tell you. Number one, I got a order here to evict you for back taxes. Num-

ber two, I got reason to believe you're harboring a fugitive name of
Alonzo Pearce. You give up Pearce, and I'll rip up the eviction order,
meaning your taxes'll be free and clear. You won't get a better deal
than that."

Shawnee shifted to draw a bead on the sheriff, just in case. This
was a setup. Teverence *did* recognize him!

Hawks hollered back. "Well, now, Sheriff, let me tell you something. Number one, you can just take your deal and shove it up the
highest part of your ass. And number two—" He raised the shotgun
and pulled back both hammers.

The sheriff abruptly dismounted and drew his sidearm at the same
time Hawks fired both barrels. The five riders scattered as two fell
from their saddles with scattershot wounds. The sheriff fired at Hawks
in the same instant Shawnee fired at the sheriff. The remaining three
men urged their horses from the scene as the sheriff dropped, struck
by Shawnee's rifle bullet.

As horses without riders ran away scared, the two wounded men
brought weapons to bear and opened fire on Shawnee's position. He
fired back two precisely aimed shots as a bullet punched through the
water barrel in front of him, barely missing him. The barrel sprung
leaks at the punctures. The two men stopped moving.

Shawnee glanced at the doorway. The chair was knocked over,
and only Hawks's legs were visible with the rest of him hidden inside
the cabin. Why had Toby Joe fired? Should have backed off and let
Shawnee handle it. Shawnee rose and looked over at the three men on
the ground. No movement. He had to check on Hawks.

Darting across to the cabin porch, he kicked the chair aside to step
in. Hawks lay on his side facing the interior. The shotgun was still in
his right hand, lying parallel to his body. Blood stained the front of
his shirt. His breathing was labored and coarse. Shawnee took a knee

beside him for a closer view at the wound. Shit! That was a killing hole. "Toby Joe!"

Hawks lifted his head with great difficulty to look at Shawnee. "Did you get 'em?"

"They're down or scattered. Why the hell'd you start shooting? Should've just hollered and got down like I told you."

Through pain and shallow breathing, Hawks attempted to answer. "Would a dropped us both. Got... jump on 'em... is all."

"Damn it, Toby Joe, what am I supposed to do for you now, way out here?"

"Nothing... I'm bad shot.... They'll bring... whole town... back.... Best you... skedaddle... 'fore they come."

"I ain't leaving you."

"Lon... you got to.... That was... the sheriff, boy.... They'll be... a-coming for you... sure now.... Don't let 'em... get you too.... D-don't—" His last breath came out abruptly and trailed off as his head dropped, hitting the floor gently.

Shawnee stared in disbelief at the passing of his friend. Even dying, he thought of Shawnee, not himself. A sick feeling rose in his stomach. He knelt there for an unknown amount of time, trying to set these two things in his mind—Toby Joe was gone, and he was responsible for it.

Maybe if he didn't come back here Toby Joe wouldn't have gotten so bold. He might've taken Teverence's offer, and he'd still be alive. And, if he didn't, he might not have resisted the sheriff, and he'd still be alive. Either way, Shawnee's being here changed things for the worse. He couldn't fix that now, but he could surely add Toby Joe to the debts Teverence owed. And he would see Teverence paid in full before he headed out.

Shawnee buried Hawks behind the cabin in a shallow grave

marked with a wooden panel reading, *Toby Joe Hawks, faithful friend.*
Carving the sign consumed a lot of time, but it was a labor of love.
From memory, he recited the twenty-third Psalm over the grave,
imagining Cletus saying it with him. Cletus would have prompted
him when he stumbled for a word here and there. "Rest easy, my
friend. I'll square it for you. Least I can do."

He returned to the cabin and packed up everything he could fit
into the saddlebags and then picked up Hawks's shotgun from where
it had fallen. Only now did he notice Hawks's last name carved into
the stock. On the way out, he pocketed a handful of shotgun shells.
"Reckon this'll deliver the proper message."

Returning to the stable, he saddled Gray, lashed the shotgun behind it, and mounted. As he rode slowly past the bodies of the sheriff
and the two posse members, he looked down at them. They'd gotten
what was coming to them. Deserved no better than to rot where
they fell. He directed Gray straight ahead toward Shawneetown.

17

THE RIDE TO THE TOWN was unhurried. There was no need to wear Gray out. Teverence wasn't going anywhere. This would be done on Shawnee's terms, in his time.

He pulled Gray up about a half mile outside the town limits. The posse men had had plenty of time to get to Teverence and fill him in. He'd figure Shawnee was coming for him, and he'd be waiting, likely loaded for bear. He'd have men all over town, laying for Shawnee. Likely the hombre siding him at Toby Joe's, clearly a hardcase, would be there as well. There was no point riding in plain as day, making an easier target. He had to play this one close to the vest.

From where Shawnee and Gray were located, they faced the main street of the town. If memory served, Teverence's warehouse was at the far end on the north side. He'd go in quiet-like, from the flank, and skirt around any traps Teverence had set up. "Let's go, Gray."

They moved slowly into some bushes and stayed hidden in the underbrush as they made their way into the town, emerging into back streets and alleyways. Shawnee hunched over in the saddle to present the smallest target. He stopped Gray behind a commercial structure. He allowed as how he was in the right place. The loading dock facing him, containing grain sacks, feed barrels and the like, suggested this was the rear of Teverence's feed and grain establishment. It was fairly new construction, as was much of the town, which was likely still rebuilding from the Quantrill attack three years earlier.

As Shawnee directed Gray toward the building, he studied the layout.

The platform was about half as tall as a horse. Big overhead door in the center and a man-sized entrance to the right. The big door likely led to the warehouse, the small door going to the office, but there was a cutout door in the big one, big enough to admit a man. That one would be his way in.

He drew rein alongside the platform and dropped the reins over Gray's head to ground tie the horse. Placing the foot closest to the platform on those planks, he lifted himself out of the saddle and onto the floor. Bending down, he whispered in Gray's ear. "Gray, wait, boy." He untied the shotgun from the bedroll, moved carefully to the small door within the overhead door, and attempted entry. It wasn't locked, but he had to be careful. The unlocking likely had been intentional-like.

The door opened easily. Shawnee stepped inside. Light was low, provided only by several large skylights in the high ceiling. As he closed the door, he took a moment to allow his eyes to become accustomed to the reduced light, then moved farther into the interior of the large facility. He went to a knee and stood the shotgun on its butt, scanning the layout in front of him.

It was a single open room with numerous support beams. There were storage ledges on either side. Each jutted about a quarter of the way out into the center and spanned the length of the building. Feed and grain items occupied most of the lower and upper spaces. Several sets of block and tackle were placed at strategic locations throughout the facility, likely for moving stuff up to and down from the ledges. The place appeared to be about forty feet long and about the same wide. The office to the right was likely an add-on, done when the place was rebuilt. He could not recall it being there when he'd been there with his father.

Teverence could be anywhere, laying for him, or maybe he wasn't there at all. Maybe his idea was to trap Shawnee in here. He would keep low and quiet, move in, and search the place.

Every sound in the huge, relatively quiet room seemed to be amplified, echoing throughout. As Shawnee moved forward, the rowels on his Texas spurs made the same slight jingling sounds they always made, but, in here, the sounds were increased many times over. He stopped and picked up some straw pieces from the floor. These he inserted between the rowels and their support bars to quell the noise. He moved on quietly, staying close to the office wall.

The wall led halfway into the space under the right hand ledge. The ledge diminished available light even more. Moving slowly forward, checking thoroughly, he reached the end of the wall. He would check the office first, then keep that behind him. He reckoned the door was around the forward corner.

Moving around the corner, he went to the door, set the shotgun against the wall, and drew his revolver. He turned the knob and pushed the door open wide. Immediately, he scanned the interior, consisting of a desk and chair and a file cabinet. Nobody there. He peered through the opening between the door and the jamb. Nothing behind the door. There was no sign of Teverence.

Shawnee closed the door quietly, picked up the shotgun, and holstered the handgun, then he moved further into the warehouse, scouring the area for Teverence. He stayed under the ledge on the right side and worked his way to the front of the building. Still nothing.

Moving quickly to the left side, he searched the area all the way to the rear. At that point, he came to the ladder leading to the upper level. He saw it to be a tough climb toting the shotgun, but he wanted the gun with him. He reached the shotgun behind him and fished the muzzle end through his gun belt so it was held against his back with the muzzle pointing down. He hoped this worked. As he moved carefully up the ladder, the shotgun hammers scraped at his back, but it was worth it to have Toby Joe with him. He scrambled onto the floor in a crouching position and pulled on the shotgun. The front sight raked his tailbone as he forced the gun up and out of its restraint.

As he stood up, the muzzle flash and loud report of a pistol shattered the quiet, echoing throughout the facility. The slug missed and bored through the wall behind him. He dropped behind a grain sack as he followed the puff of powder smoke wafting above the firing location. Shit! Teverence was on the other ledge.

Shawnee raised the shotgun and cocked both hammers. He leaned into a double blast scattering shot into the position. The powder smoke restricted his vision. Calmly, he broke the piece and extracted the empties. Then he pulled two live shells from his shirt pocket and dropped them in place. As he snapped the piece shut, a flurry of activity came from the other ledge, from the shooter's position. A figure darted from cover to the ladder on the right side and scurried down, missing several rungs.

Moving quickly to the ladder opening, Shawnee dropped the shotgun through it. As it landed below, he climbed halfway down and jumped the rest of the way, landing solidly on both feet. He picked up the shotgun and hurried across to the ladder on the other side. As he passed the ladder, one of the rungs had blood on it, and spots of blood stained the floor. Winged him. The slam of a door grabbed his attention. He turned to the office and saw the door wide open, meaning he'd made it through to the loading dock. Shawnee made a dash back to the overhead door. As he pulled the cut-in door open, Gray let out an alarmed whinny.

Shawnee stepped onto the platform to see Gray rearing and backing up. There, in the yard in front of Gray, Teverence, with his arms raised in a protective stance, backed away from the horse, then turned and ran toward the alley leading to the street. With the pistol still in his hand, Teverence had blood on his shoulder as he entered the alleyway. Shawnee had hit him all right, just not good enough. He shouldered the shotgun but had no chance for a clear shot before Teverence made it to the alley. He couldn't tell if Teverence had seen him.

Jumping off the platform, Shawnee hurried to Gray, assessing the horse's condition as he approached. Gray was all right, just protecting himself. Teverence was likely heading for help. Shawnee had to run him down, get him clear of town so he could deal with him without interference. He shoved the shotgun, muzzle first, into the bedroll and prepared to mount.

"Time to meet your maker, kid." The voice was deep and clear, and the words were measured.

It came from behind him and was not familiar. Shawnee turned quickly. The man who had been with Teverence at Hawks's place had stepped out from the alley and now rounded the loading platform. Same build, same clothes. Likely a hired gun.

In the gunman's hand, an 1858 Remington revolver was leveled and aimed straight at Shawnee's middle. "Good looking horse." Those words came through a grin. "I'll keep him after I finish you. You won't need him where you're going."

Shawnee reckoned the man was trying to rile him into making a mistake. He remembered Toby Joe advising him not to get riled. Think it through. Watch him close for an opening. Shawnee kept his hand close to his gun and moved to the side to put distance between himself and Gray. In doing this, he drew some of the man's attention, causing him to divide it between his target and the horse. Now, to get a shot at Shawnee, he had to shift his attention away from Gray, or to get to Gray, he would need to turn completely away from Shawnee.

"Quit moving." The man glanced back at Shawnee. "No place you can go." He moved a bit nearer to the horse. Shawnee knew Gray wouldn't let him get close, but the gunsel didn't know that. He needed to watch the man for the chance to move.

The gunman got too close to Gray. The horse suddenly whinnied and reared, moving toward the stranger with hooves flailing in a full on attack. The man shrank back and instinctively raised his empty hand in a gesture of protection.

Now! Shawnee grabbed the butt of his gun and whipped it out, cocking it on the fly. He dropped to one knee and fired point blank at the gunman as the man made the vain and late attempt to recover and get a shot off. Got him!

The man buckled and folded backward with a ball in his chest. He landed on his side and immediately attempted to roll into a shooting position. Shawnee's second shot ripped into the man's throat, kicking his head back sharply. His lifeless body settled back on the ground with no further movement.

Shawnee stood up and holstered his weapon. No need to check him. He wasn't coming back from that. "Whoa, boy." Shawnee went to Gray and, taking up the reins, swung up on the horse's back. They took off fast up the alley. Shawnee halted Gray sharply at the alley end and checked up and down the street.

A crowd came up the middle of the street, on the march. Out in front, Teverence led them by about ten paces.

Sure of his next move, Shawnee urged Gray forward as he pulled his rope free. He headed straight for Teverence, swinging a loop over his head. Teverence pulled back to seek cover in the crowd but could not get clear of the rope. Shawnee threw the loop forward and pulled Gray up hard. The rope settled around Teverence's chest area. Shawnee wrapped his end of the rope around the saddle horn as Gray pulled back on the rope, upsetting Teverence. He fell forward. With the rope pinning his hands to his sides, he could not break the fall. He landed hard on his face and chest, emitting an audible grunt upon impact.

The crowd kept coming as, on all sides, other people began emerging from various buildings with guns. Shawnee had to get Teverence out of here. He needed time and space to end this. Turning Gray, he started up the street, dragging Teverence face down in the dirt. If he could get him far enough away, he could get this done before they caught up to him. Keep going, Gray. A few shots sounded behind him, but nothing came close.

As they cleared the last building, Gray reached a gallop and Teverence bounced at the end of the tether. His face and chest took the brunt of the drag, scraping away skin and opening numerous wounds. A trail of blood began as dirt ground into the lesions. Teverence's screams of pain could be heard over the sound of Gray's hoofbeats and the squawks of saddle leather. Shawnee kept riding.

Glancing over his shoulder, Shawnee gauged the distance from the town to be enough to complete his task before those in pursuit could get mounted and ride after him. He pulled Gray up and turned to face Teverence who writhed in pain on the ground. "Hold him tight, Gray." The horse took a step back, taking up the slack in the rope, holding Teverence as if he were a steer.

"You know why I'm here, don't you, Teverence?"

Teverence managed to bend a leg and use his foot to turn himself on his back, but he did not answer.

Shawnee allowed Gray to move to a point where he had a better view of Teverence's face. "I asked you a question. You'd best answer up."

"Yeah, I know why."

Shawnee took a good, hard look at the mangled, bleeding face and chest and smiled. It was likely not right this felt as good as it did. "I'm curious. Did you ever have a concern about us, my family, about our lives? I want the why of it."

Teverence took a moment, likely trying to get beyond the pain. "Why?"

"I spent years building up Shawneetown, making it a decent place for folks to live. I wasn't about to let no two-bit Bushwhackers take that from me." Teverence sneered. "I'm a patriot, Pearce. You and yours are anarchists. I couldn't let you stand against me. It ain't right."

"What you done to us is what ain't right. You had no call taking the law into your own hands like you done. My pa deserved a trial, not be hung like a dog. And my ma, what about her? What she ever done to be cut down like she was? You're the cause, you son of a bitch. You made me what I be. Now it's coming back on you."

Teverence shook his head weakly. "Do what you will. Won't change nothing. You still be what you be—anarchist, outlaw."

"Yeah, one thing'll change. You be dead."

He reached behind him and pulled Hawks's shotgun from the bedroll. Mechanically, he cocked each hammer, raised the gun to his shoulder, and fired both barrels. Gray moved uncomfortably. The blasts splattered Teverence's body with lead pellets from head to chest. The body quaked as the shot hit. Then it was still. Shawnee stared at his handiwork. If he wasn't dead, he'd never be the same, but Shawnee saw Teverence wasn't breathing.

Done.

He gazed down at the shotgun, at the name on the stock. This would answer their questions. He dropped the gun on the ground, making sure the name faced up to be easily seen. He released the rope from the saddle horn and let it drop.

His peripheral vision caught movement in the distance. His attention went toward it. Riders came from town, coming after him, no doubt. There was nothing new about that. He reckoned it would go on that way till, someday, somebody got him. So, he'd keep running and maybe, just maybe, he might could help some folks along the way.

He turned Gray to the west. "Come on, Gray, time we got the hell out of here." Silhouetted by the sun against the vast, flat Kansas plains, with the townspeople in pursuit, Gray went to a gallop, taking Shawnee into the annals of Western legend.

BOB GIEL WAS BORN IN New York City and now lives in New Jersey. He has been in love with the Western genre since he was a kid, and absorbed so much of the period through books, movies, and television that he feels as though he could easily have been there himself. The grit and the determination of the people who carved a way of life out of the frontier have helped shape the way Bob lives his life. Because of that era, he keeps his word, he finishes what he starts, and he is a true friend. While he was always interested in writing, life got in the way, that is, until he retired. With the decks cleared, he began writing and never looked back.